The rider wore a scuffed black leather jacket, jeans and boots that had seen better days. He settled the bike and swung off.

Was he here to join the Easter worship service? Cassie took a step toward him. "Can I help you? We have a sunrise worship—"

The helmet came off, and a mass of silver hair sprang free. The man glanced over his shoulder, showing her his profile. A strong nose, defined mouth and firm chin. Cassie felt the breath swoosh out of her. "Peter?"

"Am I late?"

She blinked like a starstruck schoolgirl, and was instantly glad she'd had her hair stylishly cut the day before. "A bit. Did you have trouble finding the park?"

"No. Pastor Michael sent me directions. I'm sorry I'm late, but yesterday I couldn't leave work before midnight. Shall we go?"

What kind of business kept him until midnight? she wondered.

Peter took her elbow as they climbed the dirt path. For a few moments, Cassie imagined he did so because he thought her worthy of protection. That she was his to cherish. She was a little old to let herself go nutty over so inconsequential a touch.

But it was enough to dream on.

Books by Ruth Scofield

Love Inspired

In God's Own Time #29
The Perfect Groom #65
Whispers of the Heart #89
Wonders of the Heart #124
Loving Thy Neighbor #145
Take My Hand #219
Love Came Unexpectedly #286
A Mother's Promise #337
Her Cinderella Heart #353

RUTH SCOFIELD

became serious about writing after she'd raised her children. Until then, she'd concentrated her life on being a June Cleaver–type wife and mother, spent years as a Bible student and teacher for teens and young adults, and led a weekly women's prayer group. When she'd made a final wedding dress and her last child had left the nest, she declared to one and all that it was her turn to activate a dream. Thankfully, her husband applauded her decision.

Ruth's first book was published in 1993 just a month after her return to her native Missouri after years in the East. She often sets her novels in Missouri, where there are lakes and hills aplenty, and as many stories and history as people. She eagerly expects to write at least two dozen more novels.

HER
CINDERELLA
HEART
RUTH SCOFIELD

Steeple
Hill®

Published by Steeple Hill Books™

STEEPLE HILL BOOKS

Steeple
Hill®

ISBN 0-373-81267-1

HER CINDERELLA HEART

Copyright © 2006 by Ruth Scofield Schmidt

www.SteepleHill.com

Printed in U.S.A.

For God so loved the world that He gave
His only son that whosoever believes in Him
shall not perish but have eternal life.
—*John* 3:16

Carry each other's burdens, and in this way
you will fulfill the law of Christ.
—*Galatians* 6:2

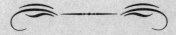

To my friend, Ruth M., who makes friends
everywhere she goes. And loves them all.

Chapter One

Why did she have to be so clumsy? She always made a spectacle of herself when she was nervous...and new situations always made her edgy.

Cassie Manning hurriedly wiped up the coffee spill under the thirty-gallon pot. She'd bumped the spigot, causing hot coffee to spatter everywhere before she'd managed to shut it off.

"Sorry," she muttered over her shoulder. The minister, Michael Faraday, affectionately known to the group as Pastor Mike, and that sleek woman who looked like the well-known model she'd been, Samantha something, stood in the church's kitchen doorway chatting. They glanced her way, but thankfully ignored the accident, intent on their conversation.

Why couldn't she just do something graceful for a change instead of her usual bumbling reactions when meeting new people? *Every new situation doesn't have to be a trial by fire, does it, Lord?*

Although her father would've said she usually made it one. He often said she must have been a changeling because neither he nor her mother had been so awkward. Nor plain, either.

Cassie shoved those negative thoughts aside. This was to be a new phase in her life. One for which she'd longed. New Beginnings, a ministry in the Blue River Valley Community Church, located in western Missouri, was exactly what she needed, with its programs on how to redirect one's life after the age of forty, and social gatherings.

Social gatherings…. The very description implied a promise that life after the first flush of youth had passed could still hold wonder and excitement.

Well, she was trying, wasn't she? She took a deep breath, steadying her nerves.

"Nothing to worry about, Cassie," Pam Lawson, a small, compact blonde standing at Cassie's side, remarked as she arranged cups and set out napkins. "That's a touchy spigot and annoys us all."

Cassie's spirits lifted. The coffee spill hadn't been entirely her fault. She grinned her thanks. She had one friend at least. "Thanks."

Pastor Mike scanned his watch, his dark lashes brushing his high cheekbones for a second before glancing their way. Although he wore a wedding ring, Cassie wondered about the status of his marriage. His wife never made an appearance at New Beginnings and Michael didn't speak of her—only his kids. She'd also overheard something the last time she was here—something negative.

Poor man. Being in the ministry was no guarantee of a happy marriage. Perhaps he needed the prayers of this group as much as the members needed his leadership, she mused. Whatever his personal problems, he'd spoken with a fine authority when he quoted Paul for this evening's scripture, and seemed to draw sustenance from it.

"Forgetting what is behind and straining toward what is ahead, I press on toward the goal to win the prize for which God has called me heavenward in Christ Jesus."

That was what Cassie was doing, pressing onward with her life. Finding new directions to what she wanted to do before her next birthday. That was what New Beginnings was all about, wasn't it? To find out what she could do with the rest of her life?

She hated thinking of her next birthday. Imagine! Next month she'd be forty years old and she'd never left home, never traveled farther than St. Louis and Branson, never had a steady boyfriend, never...

It wasn't too late, she reminded herself. She still had half her life to live, and she'd make the most of it! She just hadn't found the right man. That wasn't a crime, was it?

"Coconut cake and lemon pie," Cassie called to the group at large, urging them to come and help themselves. She hated to see the evening end, and found herself thinking about the people she met here. Her thirty-minute drive home gave her a lot of time to think about the evening. But like everyone, she had a job to face the next morning—in her case, twenty-eight fifth-graders—so she was grateful she'd be home before ten-thirty.

But it had nothing to do with who was waiting. Or who wasn't.

Her father, who'd been an invalid in a wheelchair, had died last year. So had the many demands his helplessness had made on her. She was at last free to do whatever she wanted, go anywhere she wanted, do anything she wanted. It made her feel like jumping up and down, like her fifth-graders.

That was one of the main reasons she had joined New Beginnings. She was tired of imagining drifting into old age alone.

She smiled brightly into the crowd.

Most of the nearly fifty people stood or sat in little clusters, chatting. Cassie longed to be a part of one of those clusters, but couldn't bring herself to break into one. It would be rude. After she felt more comfortable with these near strangers, then she could talk to them, she thought as she smiled. Someone might actually be interested in hearing about her day, about teaching fifth-graders. A male someone, perhaps?

But other than Pam's thanks, and several nods of appreciation for her service, no one seemed to notice her enough to invite her to join them.

Well, it would take time. Shyness wasn't a crime, after all, but she'd have to overcome it.

With a firm determination, she refilled her carafe and started the rounds again. Lovely Samantha, a former model, now stood in conversation against the wall. Why couldn't she be that beautiful? Poised? Witty?

You might as well come to terms with yourself, Cassandra. The only beauty you'll ever have is in your service to others and your obedient character....

Cassie's jaw went firm. She had to banish her father's sour voice from her head. He'd died nearly five months ago, but his hurtful opinions sometimes still invaded her thoughts.

Pastor Mike sat with another stranger, his cup sitting on the floor beside him. He often expressed himself with his hands, she'd noticed. Now he spread his fingers wide as though holding something tangible.

She could see only the back of the stranger's head, but the man's smoothly brushed hair was a lovely shade of polished silver. Silver hair….

Well, shy or not, this was the only way she knew to meet people. She headed their way, the coffee carafe in one hand and a bowl of mints in another.

Just as Cassie reached the two men, Lori Jenkens swooped past her to take a chair beside the pastor, immediately engaging him in conversation with all her considerable charm on display. But she cast flirtatious glances toward the silver-haired gentleman.

His silver mane was brushed away from his wide-set eyes like a magazine cover model, his straight nose matching his chin for strength. He was the most handsome man she'd ever seen.

Pastor Mike cast her a questioning gaze, and Cassie yanked her stare from the stranger's features. She swallowed hard, murmuring, "More coffee?" and then nearly choked while swallowing and talking at the same time.

"No thanks, Cassie," Mike answered with a smile. "I'm trying to cut down on caffeine, but I'll take some of those."

Cassie waved the dish of mints toward him. It wavered wildly in the air for a split second. Luckily, Pastor Mike grasped the dish in a firm hold.

"I'll take some," Lori said, lifting her mug. But her gaze remained fixed on the stranger. A seductive smile edged her lips.

"Mints?" Cassie asked, her mind a near blank.

"Coffee, please. Hi," Lori murmured in a throaty voice to the stranger. "I'm Lori. You're new to this group, aren't you?"

Lori wore a soft spring blouse and skirt, each following her form with loose, fluid lines. Elegant, Cassie thought in admiration as she poured. Her own figure and nondescript brown hair never excited anything beyond "that's nice" from her fellow teachers, and as for her dress, the most promising description she could ever hope for was "neat and tidy."

Cassie looked down at herself. The new skirt and blouse in shades of tan and brown were at best…serviceable.

Lori's maneuver had been fluid, too. Cassie earnestly wished she could do that. She'd have to practice that in front of a mirror.

She mentally shook herself and donned her calm teacher facade, filled Lori's cup, then turned to the silver-haired man. "How about you?"

"Sure. Thanks," he replied, throwing her a quick, uninterested glance.

At least he'd looked at her. Why would she think he'd even look at her with interest?

Why had she worn her hair in a ponytail tonight? It looked better down about her face.

Why hadn't she freshened her lipstick? She needed a new shade, she thought. She'd go shopping tomorrow after school.

His eyes were the blue of a bright summer sky, and his lashes were long and straight—just like a movie star. In fact, he was handsomer than any celebrity, she thought. He'd been out in the sun recently, too—his tan made his eyes that much more striking.

"This is Peter," Pastor Mike said, making quick introductions. "Peter Scott. And this is Lori Jenkens and Cassie Manning."

"Hello," Peter answered, his voice sounding as deep as Longview Lake. Then he addressed Lori. "Yes, this is my first visit to New Beginnings."

Cassie shivered. That voice… How could it be so like music from a bass fiddle?

"Hi," Cassie managed to squeak out as she reached for Peter's cup.

Someone moved behind their circle, and Peter shifted his weight to face Lori more squarely, listening as she chatted. Cassie was joggled. Coffee suddenly sloshed out of the pot and splattered beyond the mug, hitting Peter.

"Ugh." Peter smothered a groan and leapt up, bumping Cassie's arm. She dropped the mug. More coffee spilled. Lori and Pastor Mike scooted backward, out of harm's way.

"Oh! Oh, no…I'm so sorry," Cassie muttered, her face flushing, her free hand covering her mouth. Peter began shaking his trousers loosely to keep the fabric from his skin. "Oh, I've ruined your suit!"

It looked expensive. What if the pants couldn't be cleaned properly? Coffee stains were hard to remove.

Cassie felt helpless. How badly had he been burned? She wanted to assist him, but she hadn't even a napkin to offer.

"We've had a spill over here," Lori called to Pam in a loud voice, brushing at her skirt. Cassie felt her flush deepen and tried to ignore Lori's accusing stare.

"Are you all right?" Cassie asked Peter. She reached out to him, but then dropped her hand. What could she do? "Do you—are you burned?"

"I'm fine. Really."

Pam hurried their way with a damp cloth and a roll of paper towels. Cassie exchanged the coffeepot for the towels. She yanked one free and handed it to him.

"I'm really sorry." She felt like a dolt. Her father was right—she couldn't do much without disaster happening…. But that was nonsense. Her fifth-graders sometimes had accidents, and she always managed to remain calm throughout!

"I can get you some ice if you need it to relieve the pain—" she found herself staring at his thigh "—um…where the hot coffee burned."

"That won't be necessary." He brushed at his pants, although Cassie thought it futile at that point. "I'll live. But I lost my coffee. Suppose I can get another cup?"

"Yes. Of course. Just as soon as I get

this taken care of." She dropped to her knees, wiping the tiled floor. She bit her lip in frustration.

"At least let me pay for your cleaning," she said, staring at his shoes. They were a good brand. Very well made. But it looked as if he could stand to buy a new pair, though.

One of the men arrived with a mop, teasing her about providing him with exercise.

"Oh, yes, that was my very intention," she replied lightly, making an effort to rise to the tease. "That and making a pest of myself to Peter, here."

"Don't be silly." Peter took Cassie's elbow and lifted her to stand. His lips parted in a smile, showing even white teeth, enticing her heart to do another little skip. "I'm not hurt and the suit needed a cleaning anyway. If I'd known how informal New Beginnings is—" he glanced around the room at the many who wore jeans and sandals or sneakers "—I'd have worn my jeans, too."

"There's always next week, I suppose," Cassie offered with a hopeful tone. She glanced up at him, her heart beating a quickened beat.

"Yes, there's always next time I'm in town." The corner of his mouth edged a little wider, inviting Cassie to return a smile of her own. She felt her mouth widen. She could almost get lost in those summer-sky eyes.

Honestly, if she was imagining this man, or dreaming, she'd hide her head under a pillow from now until next year. She didn't want to wake.

Lori regained Peter's attention, and Cassie reluctantly moved away with a hidden sigh, but a lighter heart. Honestly, she had no desire to seem like an aging admirer—although with his looks, she could certainly fall into that slot. Peter could definitely qualify for adoration.

From out of town, was he? She wished she'd asked where he was from and if he was in town often.

Surreptitiously, she glanced over her shoulder. Once again she saw only the back of his head.

"An outdoor Easter sunrise service sounds wonderful to me," Cassie heard Pam say to the women clearing up. "I'm a morning person anyway, and if we have a sunrise service, then I can take my boys to see both their paternal grandparents and my mother without adding to an already crowded afternoon."

"What's this?" Cassie asked, wondering how Pam managed. Pam had both parents and two sons to fill her days. Yet her new friend couldn't have it all that easy. Pamela had lost her husband a couple of years ago. "Where?"

"Pastor Mike has secured River Bluff Park for Easter Sunday morning," Pam responded. "Providing the weather cooperates, we'll gather on the bluff just as the sun comes up. With the river below, that should be quite a sight."

"How exciting. I've never attended a sunrise service."

At the kitchen sink, Cassie turned on the tap and rinsed out the dripping cloth, thinking about the new prospect. Easter was only two weeks off.

The promise of rejoicing the Lord's victory over sin in such a wonderful outdoor setting filled Cassie with a sense of awe. In past years she'd been too confined by her father's dictates to try any church service other than their usual one. He hadn't liked his routine disturbed, and he didn't sanction any church but the one they'd attended all her life. Attendance at the usual Easter service held at a decent hour of the morning was all the Lord required of anyone, he would say.

Grumpy as he sometimes was, Cassie missed her father. He was the last of her family. There wasn't a thing wrong with the church her parents had preferred, but this year she'd make her own choices.

"The only thing we'll have to watch is the parking," Pam said. "Since the park is small, there's only a gravel clearing. We should probably organize a car pool."

"I haven't been to the park since I was a kid, so I don't know what's there. But I can help with that," Cassie offered. "What else do we need for it? Do we need to carry folding chairs? My car can carry a few."

"Each of us should bring our own lawn chairs, I guess," Pamela replied. "But I can stick an extra one or two in my van for anyone who needs one."

"Don't worry too much about chairs, ladies," Mike said, coming into the kitchen with paper plates to throw away. "I'll get some of the men to haul chairs. But we'll need some camp lights to light the drive since people will come in while it's still dark."

"Oh, yes. I hadn't thought of that," Cassie said, wiping down a counter. "And if I recall rightly, that's quite a hill up to the bluff from the parking lot, so we may need some strong arms to assist the older church members along the climb."

"That's right," Pastor Mike added.

"I can do that. I don't mind helping older people," Cassie said. The idea of the outdoor service sounded more exciting every moment. "Is there anything else to be done in preparation?"

"It's kind of you to offer, Cassie," the minister said. "We'll certainly let you know."

"Pastor Mike." Peter stood in the doorway. "I must be off. I appreciate—" he broke off, his expression closing as he realized everyone was listening. "Thanks for your help and I'll be in touch."

"Sure, Peter," Pastor Mike responded.

"No problem at all. Hey, I'll walk you out."

"Nice meeting you, ladies." Peter gave a generic nod of goodbye. Then he directed his teasing gaze toward Cassie and did a very bad Bogart imitation. "You still owe me a cup of coffee, sweetheart. With cream."

Cassie chuckled along with the others while her face went red. She could kick herself. She'd totally forgotten the coffee. "Um, anytime. You just come on along to the sunrise service on Easter Sunday and I'll buy you coffee and breakfast afterward."

"I'll see what I can do."

His smile flashed, sending her heart tumbling, and then he and Pastor Mike were gone.

"Wow, Cassie." Pam nearly chortled as she spoke. "I think you just made a date with that new guy right under Lori's nose."

"I can't believe I did," Cassie muttered, staring at the empty doorway. "I never do things like that. I'm usually too shy. Honestly, it just slipped out."

"Well, there wasn't anything mousy about that exchange," Pam insisted.

Cassie spent the next few minutes glowing. Could he be the man of her dreams?

She'd stopped dreaming of such foolish things when she'd entered her thirties, still living at home while taking care of her aging parents.

She sighed. Over the years, when all her women teacher friends talked of their boyfriends or husbands, she'd come to hate their pitying and snide secretive stares. Nearly forty and never been married….

She wasn't *that* unattractive. She'd dated a few men, but her problems at home made her less than desirable. She met very few men in her day-to-day job, also. And she just wasn't the type of woman to meet men in bars.

How likely was it that Peter would come again to New Beginnings?

No, she wouldn't count on seeing him again. Like Lori, he had a cosmopolitan air about him, as if he ran in far more sophisticated circles than the people that came to New Beginnings.

And she was about as unsophisticated as you could get, even for these parts.

No, she shouldn't really expect to see Peter again. Most likely, his parting words were only meant to make her feel better about her clumsiness.

Yet she knew, as she later entered her empty, silent house and climbed the stairs to the back bedroom she'd occupied all of her near forty years, that she'd dream of him tonight.

Peter…with the summer-sky eyes…

Chapter Two

Peter Scott Tilford flew out of the Lee's Summit airport in western Missouri at seven the next morning in his small private jet. The airport was a little small for a jet, but he'd managed. Seated beside him was his pilot, Jackson, a man who could keep his thoughts to himself and who never interfered with Peter's plans.

He'd contact his office as soon as he crossed the Appalachians, Peter thought. He'd been out of touch with his staff for three days and they'd be half frantic. No one knew where he was except his personal assistant, Tony Swartz, who was sworn to secrecy.

That was the way he'd wanted it. This was a personal matter. Very personal. News coverage and gossip about his current activities was the last thing he needed splashed all over hungry tabloid press.

He felt jubilant. After all these years, he'd hit pay dirt. Now he had to make contact.

The plane climbed to cruising altitude and Peter settled back. He'd been fortunate about not being recognized. He'd keep it that way for as long as possible, but it would take some juggling. Someone would recognize him eventually.

Private, easy, unhurried time—that was what he needed. He didn't want to scare Eric away. But in Peter's world, privacy was a highly prized commodity. Could he get it?

He'd have to carve it out carefully, but he'd do it. Take time to talk with Eric, to know the man he was sure—this side of a DNA test—was his younger brother. He wanted to do that without any outside pressures. He wanted more than five or ten minutes to become acquainted with the only remaining living person that he knew was a blood relative.

Did Eric want to know him? Be friends? Rekindle a family relationship?

Did Eric even remember he had a brother? And what were those memories?

That was the information Peter needed most.

Peter prided himself on his ability to size up a person within the first few minutes of meeting and talking with them. Many of his business decisions had been made within a very short time. He evaluated everyone involved in a project, not just the logistics. In fact, he'd earned a reputation for lightning decisions based on how he scrutinized his opponents and associates.

That was true until three days ago.

Then he'd talked to Pastor Michael Faraday. The minister had gently pointed out that in such an important matter of family, it might not be wise to make a snap judgment. Peter's ultimate decision was too important, surely, to rely on only a few minutes of acquaintance between Eric and himself. They should have had a lifetime of understanding between them; brothers should know each other well. But they'd been cheated of that.

According to the pastor, Eric was a very private man, not given to making friends easily. He had to give Eric time. Go slowly, Pastor Mike had advised.

Peter had been a teenager the last time he saw Eric. When Eric was only four, his mother, Faye, took him and fled from her marriage, from Peter's father, Randall, and everything he stood for, changing their identities along the way. He hadn't really blamed Faye. His father had created his own chaos.

After his father died, Peter expected

Eric to show up to stake a claim to his healthy inheritance, but he never had. Later, it wasn't important to wonder too closely what had happened to his brother; if Eric wanted any part in Peter's life, he would come forward. After all, Eric and Faye knew where to find him. He wasn't hiding. But he hadn't known where they could be found.

Then last year...

A familiar pain crept up like a fog. Last year Peter's only son had died of leukemia. Danny. Filled with a sorrow unlike any he'd ever known, Peter fought the tears that threatened. He felt unmanned by them, but they persisted whenever thoughts of his son surfaced. When would the pain ease?

He still grieved deeply, and guessed he always would. He'd had great hopes for Danny. Great plans.

The times he'd spent with his son were now confined to precious memories.

Danny wasn't coming back and he had to face the fact that he had no family left.

No one at all, except for Eric.

Then after months of silent suffering, he'd come out of his personal fog and finally began to look for his brother. Now he'd found him. He was elated with his hopes for a new relationship.

Yet questions haunted him. What kind of man was Eric? Did Eric grieve for his mother, Faye, who was now also dead? What had they done with their lives? Where had they lived? He wanted to know everything.

Instinctively, he trusted Mike Faraday. He'd flown to western Missouri at the suggestion of his private investigator, and set up a meeting with Pastor Mike the same day. He'd made a good choice when he decided to confide in the pastor. A good choice, indeed. Pastor Mike was a rare man of intelligence and integrity.

And Pastor Mike knew Eric. Eric Tilford—Eric Landers now. Pastor Mike had told him that Eric was a very private sort of man, but that Eric sometimes came to New Beginnings.

Sometimes he came, but not always. That was the catch.

Meeting at New Beginnings would be a neutral, nonthreatening way of sizing up Eric. Then he would know. Know what kind of man he was.

At the very least, he owed Eric his inheritance. He wanted to make it right between them, even though their separation hadn't been of Peter's making. But, buried deeply, he realized he wanted a brother.

Peter let out a deep sigh and steered his emotions away from the danger of falling into a deep well. Instead he thought about his evening.

He'd waited in edgy anticipation for Eric to arrive—and swallowed his extreme disappointment when he didn't show. Set on his course of action, he stayed long enough to seem an ordinary

visitor, listening in silence to Pastor
Mike's message, and waited another few
moment to talk with him.

He *was* getting old, he decided, to
have developed such patience. Fifty-
two. He shook his head, wondering
where the years had gone.

He didn't usually waste his time with
the kind of organization he'd attended
last night. Rather old-fashioned and
plebeian. Religious, too, which didn't
really interest him. It served other
people better, he thought.

But after a lifetime of dealing with the
inner circles of high finance and worldwide trade, and gaining acclaim for his
business savvy, it didn't hurt him, he
supposed, to see how "regular" people
lived their lives.

Take that Lori. She was smartly
dressed, mentally sharp, and she'd mentioned being an attorney. She'd fit in
anywhere. She wasn't so different from
the men and women he knew. He even

had a few women like her on staff at his law firm.

While some of the men he'd been introduced to seemed to have no interest beyond the latest fishing hole or when baseball season would start, a few, such as Pastor Mike, discussed world events along with tax problems and how to chase the moles out of one's yard. To his surprise, he hadn't been bored.

How *did* one chase moles out of one's yard? He chuckled outright because he didn't know.

"Did you say something, Mr. Tilford?"

"No, Jackson, just thinking," he replied. "Say, did you ever have occasion to chase moles from your yard?"

"Moles? No, sir. I live in an apartment."

"Never mind. Just an idle thought."

"Yes, sir."

He fell silent again, and his thoughts

returned to the company he was in the night before.

There had been that moment of comedy—right out of a slapstick movie—when Cassie spilled the coffee. Usually, he had no patience with careless waitresses—but Cassie wasn't a waitress. She was a guest at that meeting just as he was. He'd surprised himself when he felt no ire and recognized her act of kindness for what it was when she freshened his coffee.

She certainly hadn't known who he was. The only person he had to be careful of was that ex-model, Samantha. She might recognize him.

He suspected Cassie was a quiet woman. Her brown skirt, beige blouse and sensible shoes certainly held no spark or style. Yet unlike Lori's sophisticated flirtation, Cassie's green eyes had returned his gaze with an undisguised interest that was as easy to read as the newspaper. Her gaze was guileless.

Something he saw there flattered him, just a little.

He'd enjoyed the surprise on her face when he did his very bad Bogart imitation, something he hadn't done since his college days. He'd even laughed at himself for doing it.

Surprisingly, he'd actually had fun for those few moments. There had been very little to tickle his amusement in the past few years. Certainly not since Danny had passed away.

Why now? Why something so simple?

Perhaps it had been too long since he'd seen genuine interest from a woman for simply being a man. No frills, no expectations, just a thread of plain attraction.

He switched his cell phone on, and two seconds later it rang. Automatically, he reached for it. His incognito jaunt had come to an end and his business agenda and calendar demanded his immediate attention. "Yes?"

"Peter! At last!" Tony's frustration made his tone gruff. "I've been calling you for hours."

"Don't sweat it, Tony. I'll be there in time for our lunch meeting with Carter and Jones...."

It came to him as a certainty. He'd be back to the eastern edge of Kansas City, Missouri, for sure. New Beginnings met each week and he'd arrange to be there often enough to meet Eric, and to discover if Eric wanted to know him. He'd rather enjoyed his time spent there. Being anonymous was a new experience. Why shouldn't he have a little fun?

Just after noon, Cassie grabbed her blue canvas lunch bag and thankfully headed toward the teacher's lounge. Fridays the kids were always fidgety in anticipation of the weekend, and today was no exception. The weekend promised to be beautiful. They'd been so restless today she felt like tearing out her hair.

Rico was the worst—he couldn't sit still nor keep himself quiet for more than five minutes. He agitated the other children around him on purpose.

Cassie liked the boy, and thought he needed only a little more personal attention at home. But his mother had five others at home, a busy husband and no extra time to give Rico.

If Cassie had to call Rico's mother one more time…

She'd have to pray and think about it, Cassie decided as she swung open the teacher's lounge door and plopped her bag on the table. Maybe she could find another way to help Rico.

"Hey, Cassie," Jacqueline, who taught sixth-graders, greeted from the cola machine. "Did you get that notice on the visiting Oregon Trail historian for next week?"

"Hi. Yeah, I have it." Cassie grimaced

at Jacqueline's lunch plate from the cafeteria and dug into her bag for her tuna sandwich on whole wheat. "I thought I'd do some reading over the weekend to refresh my memory of trail lore. Couldn't hurt to be prepared."

"Not me," Liz Dapple remarked, scooping cottage cheese into her full, perfectly shaped mouth. Her quick glance held a bit of the usual withering pity for anyone who took their job too seriously. "I don't plan on wasting my time on anything related to kids, school, clocks or bells. I'm going to have a luxurious dinner and a cuddle with my honey, a shopping spree tomorrow, and then a long Sunday in the park."

A cuddle with someone loved. Cassie could picture the romantic thought.

"My weekend won't contain anyone who doesn't stand taller than me, either," Amanda Smith remarked with a grin. "I do have to clean house, though.

And then Dwayne and I are going to a concert with friends."

A concert with friends. That sounded fun….

"Wish I could say the same," Donna chipped in with a sigh. "But it's an animated feature film for us with our kids tonight, then after some major laundry tomorrow, my hubby and I are working in the yard."

"By the time I leave here on Fridays I've had enough of smart-mouthed kids," Jacqueline said. Still in her twenties, she'd just graduated from college, and had come to the school as a substitute. "I'm going to a friend's party down in Westport and I'll hopefully meet some cute guys."

"My boy Derrick and I are heading to Branson just as soon as the final bell rings," Farley, the band teacher, said. He brushed a hand over his balding head, tapping a rhythm on his forehead. "Do a little fishing on Table Rock Lake, then take in a music show, maybe."

Dinners, concerts, parties. It was a repeat of the litany Cassie heard every weekend, every holiday and vacation. What Cassie wouldn't give to have what Donna had—a husband and family of her own.

"Mmm…" Her sigh sounded more like a groan. Several pairs of eyes turned her way.

"Um, I—" She shoved a pickle chip into her mouth, and mumbled, "I'm going to a—a—"

She didn't want to call it a Bible Study. This group already thought her an immense Goody Two-shoes, and except for Donna, who was a believer like herself, most of them didn't understand her love of Godly things and her eager spiritual journey.

Goody Two-shoes. She was so tired of that tag. Besides, she couldn't bear another pitying glance over her reports of another quiet weekend spent alone.

"A Friday night thing at a friend's house, then maybe an outing on Sunday afternoon with…um, someone new in my life."

Peter came to mind, with his silver hair and his eyes the color of a summer sky. They made her insides all shivery. Cassie stopped chewing while she drifted off.

Amanda gave her a curious stare. "Cassie?"

"Someone new?" Jacqueline asked, raising a doubtful eyebrow.

"Uh—you could say that." Cassie let a smile form, then picked at the remainder of her sandwich.

"Do tell," Amanda begged.

"Cassie has a boyfriend?" Jacqueline sounded just too incredulous. It set Cassie's back up.

"*Why* is that so surprising?" she wanted to know, her sudden heated look defying

Jacqueline to add another remark. Then she turned to answer Amanda. "It's too soon. There's nothing to tell."

Then slanting a mysterious glance at Jacqueline, she let her mouth curve. "Yet…."

Now what was she doing? Implying something that wasn't there. Lying, Dad would call it. But she had met a gorgeous man, and he had smiled an incredible smile at her. She had exchanged conversation with him. She did hope to see him again, didn't she? It wasn't a lie.

She ruthlessly pushed Peter out of her thoughts. She should do something about Rico, something practical, that's what she should be thinking about.

She'd call Rico's mother and ask to take Rico and his two older sisters to see the National Trails museum in Independence. From the last time she'd talked to Mrs. Sanchez, she thought the harried woman would welcome the suggestion.

That should give them all an outing, and it sure would beat having to make another complaining call.

However, to set things straight…

"Then again," she spoke up in a decisive tone, "I have a different interest in another direction, too. So perhaps Sunday will turn out…oh, you know."

Rico couldn't be counted on to remain quiet about the excursion if they went, but she'd chance it. His two sisters were already in middle school; they were unlikely to rat on her.

"Two guys? Cassie, you flirt!" Liz teased.

Heat climbed Cassie's cheeks. "Not really two. The one isn't really dating material. But I'm not sure if my first choice will be in town."

"It's about time you met someone new," Donna kindly remarked as she got up from the table to throw trash away. "What's he like?"

Much too good-looking for comfort.

"Who's the dreamboat?" Jacqueline asked.

"Oh, just someone…" Cassie mumbled, then caught herself. She spotted Donna giving the young substitute a quelling stare, pity lying in the depths of Donna's brown eyes. Oh, no! They were doing it again!

Cassie cleared her throat and lifted her chin. "As for *Peter*—" she boldly named him. She didn't know if she'd ever really see him again, but at least he was real. "I honestly don't know yet. We're merely at the exploring stage."

"Well, at least tell us—is he cute?" Liz asked.

"Mmm, is he ever! He has eyes that are so blue…."

Chapter Three

Stars twinkled in the velvety heavens as Cassie reached the dark River Bluff parking lot Easter morning. It was barely 5:00 a.m. Several male figures, momentarily unidentifiable, were unloading chairs from a truck. One paused to peer at her.

"Cassie?" Pastor Mike's voice floated her way.

"Yes, it's me." She hugged her blue wool jacket closer against the morning chill as she got out of her car. Her lined slacks felt comfortable for now, but she suspected she'd be glad to change them to something lighter by the time she returned home midmorning. "Can I help?"

"Sure can. Come hold this lantern high so we can see what we're doing. We've a number of metal garden hooks to hold our lanterns, but we have to get them into the ground. As soon as we have more lights hung, it won't be so dark along this rocky path."

Cassie grabbed the camp lantern and held it high above her head. Another truck arrived with more chairs and more people. Pam and her two teenage boys piled out, saying hi, and then setting to work. As the tall garden hooks were inserted into the ground every few yards, Cassie traipsed back and forth from the truck to wherever a lantern was needed.

Pam joined her in hanging lanterns as the men passed them along the way. Cassie enjoyed the camaraderie the work created. Soft voices rose in greeting as people arrived, a few calling to tease, some offering encouragement along every step on the path, some making reverent remarks. Finally, the metallic sound of unfolding chairs ceased. Above, the chairs were set in a semicircle facing east.

Cassie, as directed, stationed herself about a third of the way up the path, where a sharp turn might create a difficulty for an older worshipper. Pam was just above her, shivering.

"I hope it warms up in the next hour," Pam remarked. "It's chillier than I expected."

Cassie agreed, pulling gloves from her pocket. "I remembered to bring a blanket, just in case I might need one. Seems we'll definitely need one."

Pam swung her torso around to rev up her circulation. "I did, too, but the boys have them."

"You can share mine if you want," Cassie offered.

"Thanks. I suspect I'll need it."

As the sky lightened, more people streamed by on their way to the top of the bluff. Most were young twentysome-things, a number were teens and a few were families with older children. Less were older, but Cassie and Pam cheer-fully leant an arm to those who needed it up the stone-filled path. Thankfully, Cassie noted that many carried a blanket or throw against the chill.

Cassie gazed up the hill when she heard the first chords of a keyboard. A lovely soprano voice began to sing a joyous song, and then an alto joined in.

"We should go," Pam said, her head turned toward the music. They couldn't see the singers, but their floating voices sounded wonderful. "They're starting."

Glancing downhill, Cassie saw the parking lot was not only filled, but overflowed. And there seemed no one left to arrive.

"Okay. Go ahead," she said over her shoulder, starting downhill. "I'll be there just as soon as I get my blanket out of my car."

A low roar reached her as Cassie opened her trunk to pull out the old navy blanket she used for picnics. A moment later, a heavy black motorcycle drove up into the lot and stopped. The motor shut off.

The rider wore a scuffed black leather jacket, jeans and boots that had seen better days. He settled the bike and swung off, his hands going up to his helmet.

Cassie closed her trunk, hugging the blanket close to her chest. Was he here to join the worship service or had he stopped for another purpose? This was a public park and the rider might not know that it was in use.

Perhaps he'd like to join the service anyway. She took a step away from her car. "Can I help you? We have a sunrise worship—"

The helmet came off, and a mass of

silver hair sprang free. The man glanced over his shoulder, showing her his profile. A strong nose, a defined mouth, a firm chin and a lock of gorgeous hair over a dark brow. Cassie felt the breath swoosh out of her. "Peter?"

"Am I late?"

"A bit." She blinked like a starstruck schoolgirl, instantly glad she'd taken the plunge to have her hair stylishly cut and highlighted the day before. It fluffed on top, but clung at the neck. It made her look at least five years younger. "Did you have trouble finding the park?"

"No. The map and directions Pastor Mike sent me were good."

Pastor Mike sent him a map?

"Then you must have come a long way this morning."

"Actually, I did." He gave a half-hearted grin. "Had some business to wrap up that kept me up till midnight two nights running, and then yesterday, I couldn't leave before late in the day.

Shall we go?" His attitude was as if it were nothing. He gestured toward the lit path as the sound of the entire congregation in song drifted down.

What kind of business kept him until midnight?

"Sure. I was just going up, but came back for my blanket."

"Let's go, then."

He took her elbow as they climbed the dirt path. For a few delirious moments, Cassie imagined he did so because he thought her worthy of protection. That she was his to cherish. It was little enough to dream on, she reminded herself, a simple act of kindness. Yet she was a little old to let herself go nutty over so light a touch. And a gloved touch, at that.

Still, she let herself enjoy it.

Cassie pulled her swirling thoughts around to concentrate on the service and pointed out two empty chairs next to Pam at the rear of the crowd. They made their way to them.

A finger of sunlight shafted over the horizon as they sat down, and she felt her spirit lift high with the light and celebration. Without thought, she spread her blanket over her cold legs, distributing the ends to Pam and Peter on either side of her. Peter gave her a sideways glance, his mouth slightly tilting as he accepted his end.

Resolute, Cassie focused her gaze forward.

Christ our Lord is risen today.... A quartet reminded them in the old, meaningful song, then urged all to join.

Lord, how grateful I am to be here this day. To worship You on a hilltop. It is the greatest reminder....

Pastor Mike began his sermon. Behind him, the sunlight slowly pushed back the night. For one brief moment, a single ray lit Pastor Mike's face.

A fitting picture, Cassie thought. There's nothing more completely dreadful and altogether beautiful than the recounting of the resurrection story. That terrible black day, turned to three. Then glorious victory…Christ's victory over evil when He rose from death, and His salvation made available for us all through faith….

Cassie's heart swelled with that hope and faith. Beside her, she felt Peter grow still. Listening. Taking it all in, every word. How long had it been since he'd heard the story? Had he ever, she wondered? Or perhaps never to the point of belief?

She had no way of knowing what Peter believed. She didn't know where he was in his own walk with the Lord, or if he'd even begun one, but she suddenly felt the need to offer up a silent prayer for him. Something about him stirred her in a way beyond the obvious attraction.

Lord, speak to him now…. Let his heart be ready….

She shouldn't be so aware of him— but she was. It wasn't fair that he distracted her when she didn't want to be distracted. She barely heard the close of the service.

They rose for one last song and Pastor Mike's gentle benediction.

"Thanks for sharing, Cassie," Pam said, folding her end of the blanket into Cassie's hands.

"Yeah, thanks," came from Peter as he, too, stood and stretched. His tone dropped to a low growl. "It was very nice of you. Excuse me, please. There's someone I need to see."

"You're welcome," Cassie replied, trying not to watch him walk away. Trying not to let her disappointment of his quick abandonment show.

Cassie admonished herself. How could she feel abandoned when she barely knew the man? Besides, she'd had his company for the whole service, hadn't she?

Pam stretched to her toes to scan the worshippers. "Now where did my boys get to? Can you see them? They promised to help carry chairs back. Then we're off to see their dad's parents. They don't get out much anymore, and I try to get the boys over to see them about every week."

"I think they're over there." Cassie pointed to the outer edge of the crowd where a clutch of teens stood.

"So they are. Okay. See you later."

Cassie finished folding the blanket, gathered her purse and glanced at her watch. It wasn't even eight-thirty, and the whole day stretched before her.

She could go to another Easter service. A more traditional one. Perhaps in the church where she and her father had gone. Yet that had little appeal.

"Are you going for breakfast?" Cassie overheard someone ask another worshipper. A woman with a family in tow, she noted.

"Yes, are you coming? We're meeting at Chase's, but we have to leave there no later than ten. Bill's folks are doing dinner, it takes us an hour to drive it, and they don't like us to be late."

Cassie hid a sigh. This was when she missed her parents most. She had no one left to spend holidays with. No one to ask her to dinner on Easter, or any special days. Yet she was taking steps to make new friends, wasn't she? She'd joined New Beginnings. And she found it exciting and stimulating, both spiritually and in other ways.

She looked around now as the crowd trooped down to the parking lot. Perhaps there were others who were as alone as she who wanted to spend the day together.

Recognizing Lori, Sam Talent and Bonnie Sentry from the New Beginnings bunch, she edged toward them. Perhaps they'd want to go for breakfast if they didn't have other plans.

Before she could reach them, Cassie saw Lori make a beeline toward Peter and

Pastor Mike, a bright smile spreading across her perfectly made-up face. Cassie stopped in her tracks. Should she continue? Lori might not like her interfering.

Peter, his face wearing a blank expression, nodded at something Pastor Mike said as the two men turned and started slowly from the clearing.

Cassie started forward again.

"Well, good morning, Peter," Lori greeted in a delighted voice. "It's very good to see you this morning. A bunch of us are heading to breakfast at Dude's, in Westport. Why don't you come along?"

Cassie stopped once more. Waited. She wished she was bolder, like Lori, but she couldn't bring herself to insinuate herself on Lori's invitation. Disappointed, she turned to head down the pathway.

A hand clamped her shoulder and, startled, she glanced up. Peter had stopped her?

Cassie's heart started pounding. Peter's flashing glance held a teasing command before returning to Lori.

"Sounds good to me," Peter answered. "I missed my coffee this morning, and this woman owes me one. Don't you, um…?"

His arm slid around her shoulders and Cassie stood perfectly still. In awe and wonder.

"Cassie," she reminded in a murmur, her heart beating like a kettledrum.

"Are you free?" he muttered into her ear. His breath tickled her skin, and she caught a hint of expensive cologne. "Please say yes."

"Yes." She was being used as a rescue date, but it didn't matter. Saying no was *not* an option!

Peter raised his voice to answer Lori. "Yeah, thanks. Cassie and I will join you."

Cassie had no idea if Lori was pleased at her inclusion or not. She was too busy staring at Peter. She heard Lori's answer as a faraway bell, but couldn't have repeated what Lori had said if offered a thousand dollars.

"Do you know the place they're going?" he asked with a quick wink. He slid his hand to her elbow.

"I can find it." Oh, her voice was actually *quivering*. He'd think her an absolute freak.

"Where is it?"

"In Westport."

At his blank look, she explained further. "Westport is a historical district in Kansas City. Near the Country Club Plaza. It's a popular hangout on weekends for the, um, with-it people."

"Ah." He nodded, a gleam of understanding in his eyes. No doubt he was familiar with such places, Cassie thought.

Cassie had never been to any of the popular spots on a Saturday night. Dude's was well known to draw the older singles crowd. A Sunday morning wouldn't match what she imagined it to be like then, but she was curious enough to see it.

Several men carried the same chairs down that they'd carried up just two hours before. Cassie spied a box of song sheets, and picked it up to take down to the trucks.

"Are you coming, Pastor Mike?" Peter folded the few chairs he stood near, then hoisted a stack to carry.

"Not this morning, Peter," Pastor Mike said. "I only have a couple of hours before our formal church service begins, and I must go home to change. Maybe next time."

"Later?" Peter queried.

"How about tomorrow? Call the office," the minister suggested. "I'll be there early."

"Good. I'll do that."

Cassie briefly wondered what the two men had to talk about, but she let the thought go. Then her thoughts swirled on the date she'd suddenly acquired. She was to have *breakfast with Peter*....

The parking lot rapidly cleared out as Peter helped load the equipment. Cassie ran back up the hill to scan the area for any trash that may have been left, then hurried back down.

Peter pulled on his leather jacket and reached for his helmet. He reminded her of a knight putting on his armor before a jousting tournament.

"Would you like to ride with me?" he asked.

Cassie paused, her car key hovering above her car door. Her mouth dropped and she felt her eyes widen. On the bike?

The motorcycle suddenly seemed to grow like a giant black insect, frightening in its unfamiliarity and remembered roar. She'd be forced to put her arms around his waist for safety...and...and hug him. The thought of climbing on the back of that monster and embracing

Peter, of placing her cheek against his back as they rode, sent her into cascades of excitement.

"Are you serious?"

He ran an evaluating glance at her skirt and blouse, and then studied her face. "Actually, not this time. I have an extra helmet, but you should be wearing something more protective if we're going very far."

"You could ride with me," she offered, swallowing her disappointment. Would she really have the nerve to ride on that thing?

That was her trouble, she admonished herself, and the very thing she'd promised herself to change. She'd never been very adventurous when it came to new experiences. Furthermore, her handful of high school dates had done little to prepare her for adult men.

"Don't think that would be a good idea, do you? Leaving my bike in a park unattended for hours."

Now was a good time to be bolder. She took a breath and said, "I don't live too far from here. You can leave it in my drive. It would be safe there."

"That would work." He gave an accepting smile. "Lead the way, my lady."

My lady. Just like a knight in a romantic novel.

Getting into her car, she sighed. Boy, would she have something exciting to tell her teacher friends when school resumed after Easter break. Even if this was only a one-time thing and she never saw Peter again. Even if this was only a pity date.

Glancing through her rearview mirror as she pulled onto the road, she made certain that Peter followed.

He waved. She smiled. Pity date, or not, she'd take it and be happy.

Chapter Four

Most of the group was already seated at Dude's when she and Peter entered. The place hadn't quite become crowded yet.

"Hi, you two. Come on and sit down," said Dennis.

"What kept you, anyway?" asked Lori, curiosity showing all too plainly. "We've already ordered."

"Had to park one of the vehicles," Peter muttered as he held the chair for Cassie, then slid into the chair beside her. He picked up a menu. "Is the food good here?"

Cassie made herself more comfortable and wondered the same, since she'd never patronized the place. But she was more interested in her surroundings. "Hi, everybody. Sorry about the delay, but I'm glad we didn't keep you from waiting to order."

The talking and teasing continued. Their food came a few minutes later, and they ate with happy chatter. Under the noise, Lori asked, "What are all of you doing the rest of the day?"

"Well, I've got a bit of work," Peter started.

"On Sunday?" Lori interrupted. "This is a holiday, Peter. You're not allowed to work today."

"Yeah, it's Easter Sunday, buddy, haven't you heard?" said Dennis. "We're celebrating the risen Lord. No work allowed today."

Peter glanced around the company. Then he chuckled offhandedly. "Well, what are you all doing today? Going to a museum? Or a movie? Or to another church function?"

"No, we don't go to church all the time," said one of the men with a grin. "I'm expected at my son and new daughter-in-law's later. Gotta be the gracious father-in-law, y'know. Maybe if you want to meet tonight, I'd go. But not this afternoon."

"Why don't you all come to my apartment?" Lori quickly counted heads. "It's tiny, but we could all squeeze in. We can play music, or watch TV. Then later we can go out for dinner."

"Hey, that sounds cool," stated one of the women. "But I gotta go have dinner with my folks. And then to my ex in-laws' to pick up my kids. Wade's old enough to drive these days, but I have the car."

The restaurant was filling up, now, and the crowd began to break up. Dennis said, "I'll come, Lori."

"How about you, then, Peter? And, um, Cassie, of course."

Peter glanced at Cassie, half smiling. An enticing smile, it was intended to let their companions suspect they were already busy. Together. It made Cassie a bit uncomfortable. "No, I don't think so this time. We have plans of our own," Peter said.

Cassie thought Lori would see her heart beat underneath her dress, it pounded so hard. But she managed to sputter, "Um, yes, we sure do." She pulled her gaze away from Peter with an imaginary crowbar. "Please excuse us. But we'll see you at the next New Beginnings meeting."

Cassie couldn't believe she'd been so bold—again! There was no guarantee she'd ever see Peter once more, much less expect him to be at New Beginnings. But after they said goodbye, she led him to her car with confidence.

"That was nice. I usually eat breakfast

alone." She talked for something to say as she unlocked the car.

"Oh?" He scooted into the passenger seat. "I don't usually eat anything until noon. Just coffee to keep me going."

She turned the ignition key, and started out of the parking lot. "Breakfast is the most important meal, haven't you heard?"

"I might have heard somewhere," he said, smiling.

"Do you really have to work this afternoon?" She glanced at him before she pulled the car into the street.

"Yeah, I do." He yawned, then apologized for it. "I'm sorry, but I didn't get in till late last night."

"Not much sleep, huh. That's too bad."

Peter was quiet for most of the ride home. Cassie thought he'd fallen asleep, but he was just sitting in the passenger seat, staring at the passing scenery, pensive.

Thirty minutes later, she pulled into her driveway.

"We're here."

Peter woke from his daydream and looked around. "Where? Oh, yeah. Your house."

His cell phone rang as he unbuckled his seat belt. He automatically reached into his inner pocket, flipping the phone open as he brought it to his ear. "This is Peter…."

Cassie slowly slid from her seat. He hadn't exited her car, but sat with the door open, his feet on the ground. His elbows rested on his knees.

He raised to sit straight, exclaiming, "He was there?"

She heard him grumble, "I can't believe it. I'm at the service, and he's actually there, and I didn't know? Sure, sure. Can't be helped any, but…"

He listened for a moment. "Yeah. I will. No, I don't think—"

Peter glanced at Cassie, then continued talking on the cell phone. "Look, I'm going to be out of town till next weekend. I can come then. You'll keep in touch?"

He sighed with a slight frown as he closed his cell phone and slipped it back into his pocket. He gazed down at the driveway, thinking. His expression held a bit of defeat.

"Not bad news, I hope?"

"No, it's nothing I can't handle. Just a delay." He rose and seemed to shake off his doldrums. "I've got to go. Thanks, Cassie. It's been a great morning."

"Yes, it's been nice."

They walked back to his motorcycle, and he pulled his helmet out, putting it on. Then he climbed on the bike. "See you."

Cassie nodded, feeling a shot of disappointment. She hoped to see him again, but she had no guarantee. Then Peter roared out of her drive without a backward gaze.

Cassie tucked her disappointment away, out of sight and not to be thought of again. Disappointments were old friends to Cassie, and she kept them buried in the basement. She had a class of children to teach and prepare for, and she had no time to feel sorry for herself.

Twelve days later, Cassie sat with Pam in a regular meeting of New Beginnings, singing for all she was worth to the Lord.

Someone sat down next to her. Peeking from the edge of her eye, she almost lost her voice when she saw it was Peter. He nodded with half a grin, and waited for the song to end.

It was a Thursday, the regular New Beginnings night. What was Peter doing here?

He'd sat down next to her. When there were at least—she quickly made a survey of the room—ten other chairs he could have chosen. Her spirits lifted.

The music over, Pastor Mike stood

and began the teaching. "We're in Hebrews tonight, folks. The New International Version, continuing our study on faith. Hebrews eleven." He was quiet a moment, then started to read. "Now faith is being sure of what we hope for and certain of what we do not see…this is what the ancients were commended for."

Automatically, Cassie opened her Bible. The rustle of pages around her told her others did the same. She noticed Peter sat with his hands in his lap. He had well-shaped hands, well cared for. These were not hands that did manual labor.

She remembered them.

"Here," she whispered, shoving the opened Bible at him.

Peter's blue eyes flashed her way, then he reached for the left edge of the book. It meant leaning closer…and Cassie breathed deeply. A faint scent emanated from him, something she couldn't name, but recalled from nearly two weeks ago.

Pastor Mike continued to follow Hebrews and how the ancients held on to their faith through hardship and even death. It meant a lot to Cassie, the thought of hanging on to her faith throughout life, no matter what happened. It had sustained her through the loss of her parents, all the petty and major events of school, of her lonely life.

When the final prayer ended, Peter whispered, "Catch you later," and stepped away. Cassie watched him as he approached Pastor Mike, his long fingers brushing back his thick silver hair. Stifling her sigh, she rose and went to the refreshment table to help dispense dessert.

But she couldn't keep from watching Peter. Glancing up at them as she set out cookies, she saw Pastor Mike nodding toward the opposite side of the room. Peter turned to look.

Her gaze flew there, too. It was only Eric Landers, by himself, watching a group of women. Another poor soul, she thought.

She looked over at Peter again. He stared at Eric, rock still. Eric was preparing to leave, talking to no one, paying attention to no one. Peter slowly moved to intercept him.

"Are there any sugar-free cookies tonight?" asked Barbara Edwards.

"Um, I think so." Cassie turned to Pam. "Sugar-free cookies?"

"Yeah, this plate has them. Here you go, Barbara."

Someone asked for hot tea. She followed through with the request. By the time she looked back, the two men had disappeared. Where had they gone?

The newlyweds, Lisa and Ethan Vance, came in amidst much ado, then chatted about the steady customers at their restaurant. Lisa looked radiant.

"I'm surprised you could get away," remarked Beth Anne Hostetter, one of the associate pastors.

"It's after nine," Lisa remarked. "The restaurant is closed. But we can't stay. We have to get home to the children."

"How are you managing married life with working together?" asked Pam.

"Remarkably, it's working out beautifully," Lisa replied, casting a glance at her husband. A look of total love. "But we're so busy with the four children, Uncle Fred and the restaurant, we haven't had much time for New Beginnings. We thought we'd stop by to say hi to everyone. We miss you."

The love that shone from Lisa's gaze had Cassie wistfully envying all that togetherness. What would it be like living with children and a husband?

Well, in truth, as a teacher she knew what living with children would be like. What she really wished for…

She dropped her gaze. It was better that she stick to what she knew—helping others. But she drew a deep breath, full of hope.

* * *

"I suppose you don't remember me, do you, Eric?" Peter spoke softly. His stomach clenched into a knot. His companion pulled his light-gray jacket on, preparing to pick up his Bible.

Eric glanced up with the same dark eyes as his mother. It startled Peter a bit. Did Eric know he looked like his mom? "Should I? I'm sorry, no…."

Peter remembered those eyes. Big and widely spaced, they almost swallowed the rest of his face. "I'm Peter…."

"Nice to meet you, Peter." Eric nodded, then prepared to leave.

"Aren't you staying for coffee?"

"Nah…don't drink the stuff."

"I wish I didn't. I drink too much of it. I suppose the social hour doesn't interest you, either?"

Eric glanced about the room, as though looking for someone. Or as though he didn't know what Peter might want of him.

"Not tonight. Got a wounded patient at home to take care of."

"A wounded patient?"

"Um, a bird with a broken wing."

The light exchange of words served to relax Peter a bit. He rarely recalled ever being so uptight. He usually was in charge of situations.

"Oh. Well, I'd like to talk with you, if I may?"

Eric's glance was surprised. "What about?"

After glancing about the room, Peter suggested, "Perhaps we could go somewhere more private."

A suspicious glint entered Eric's gaze. He tipped his head. "Suppose you tell me what this is about?"

Eric's eyes questioned, and Peter wanted to ease into his introduction. "I will. But not here."

Eric studied Peter's face, curiosity in his eyes.

"I suppose we can go outside," Eric

said slowly. "There's a bit of a garden by the side of the church."

The garden was a small space that had rows of tulips, daffodils and crocus, which were all beginning to bloom. A bench sat in front, inviting a person to sit there and enjoy the garden. Pastor Mike had told him how nice it was.

"Lead the way," Peter said.

Eric turned and walked from the big open room. Outside, the sound of the crowd's chatter subsided. He stood for a second in silence, gazing at the parked cars in the lot, then turned to the side of the church. His shoes made no sound on the grass, then a crunch as he stepped onto a small graveled oval with a bench in the middle. Tall trees beginning to bud sent out a fragrance. The corner light on the church cast the area in shadowed beams.

Here Eric turned. "Okay, now. What is it? What do you want?"

Peter shoved his hands in his pocket, staring at Eric's face. Impatience shone from his eyes. Was there no recognition? No remembrance of piggyback rides or sneaked cookies and milk shared in the large kitchens?

"I— Do you remember anything about your earliest childhood?"

Eric frowned. This came out of the blue for him, and all of a sudden he was cautious. "No. Not much. Why?"

"Your mother was Faye Perkins, wasn't she?"

Silence met Peter's question. Then a surly, "Yes, she was. What about it?"

"I knew her."

"You did, huh? So? What do you want with me? If she owes you money or something, you can go bother another guy. I don't have any and I don't know where she is."

Startled, Peter said, "No, she doesn't owe me money. I just wondered what happened to her son."

"Well, here I am. But I'm not open to a sentimental reunion or anything like that. You can push that idea right out of your head." His hand went out, making a slicing motion. "I want nothing to do with her or any of her…er, activities or involvements."

"Her activities are nonexistent," Peter said slowly, softly, and with a pain he didn't understand. He hadn't thought of Faye in years. "She died over twenty years ago."

Eric was silent a long moment. He made no movement, processing the information, his eyes on the bench. There was no sign of grief. "I was in the Navy twenty years ago. I haven't seen her since I was seven."

This was much worse than Peter thought. He hadn't imagined Eric would be hostile. Or ignorant of at least some of the facts. He wished he could see Eric's expression in better light, but the beams from the corner cast too many shadows. "Didn't she ever contact you? Write or call?"

"Nah. She disappeared as soon as she left me with a foster family."

"A foster family? But you knew where your father was, surely?"

"Nope. Only have vague recollections of him. She told me he died."

"Well, yes, he's gone now." But not for a few years after Faye had left him.

Eric studied Peter with a bitter gleam shining through his gaze. He didn't ask how Peter knew his parents, his family, how he knew of both Faye's and his father's death. He didn't ask anything at all.

"So now you've told me. Well, I'm not better off with the knowledge, I can tell you that. It doesn't affect me. But you've done your duty." Eric took a deep breath, then said, "My childhood in foster homes was…fine, it was tolerable. My life in the Navy was better. Now I'm out, and I like my life just fine. Thanks."

He walked away with long, quick strides.

Chapter Five

Peter almost didn't go back into the building. He'd never suffered stark rejection like that before. Like a door slammed in his face. His sadness was real and hurt like blazes. But he owed his thanks to Pastor Mike, and he thought he'd offer him a word or two before he left. He also needed advice on the best way to leave Eric the money he was due.

He walked back in, wiping the defeat from his face. He turned his mind to the tasks of the next day. The Johnson-Cicero deal was due tomorrow, and he wanted to look over the papers once more. Make sure he had all his i's dotted and his t's crossed. He wanted to fly down to the Virgin Island property, as well. He had things to do, and he had no more time to spend here.

Glancing about, he saw Pastor Mike involved with a couple of people. The man was busy and, letting out a sigh, he thought perhaps he'd just leave. A note would have to do.

As he turned to leave, he ran into Cassie. Here was one person who accepted him, no questions asked. And she hadn't a clue as to who he was or the financial power he wielded.

Neither did Eric, he thought.

The knowledge that Eric didn't know who he was hit him with full force. He couldn't just leave it! He had a brother, and before this was done, Eric would know him. Know him as a loving brother. If rejection came with that full knowledge, then so be it.

The knowledge brought him considerable relief. His mood lightened immediately.

Cassie brought a smile to his face. He reached to touch her shoulder, a technique he'd used often in business, yet he did it naturally now. He wanted to reassure her that he'd see her again. "It's been fun, Cassie. New Beginnings is growing on me. I'm off now. Gotta be in New York early tomorrow."

"New York?" Her eyes grew as big as saucers.

Peter could have bit his tongue. Why had he let that slip out?

He let his grin spread flirtatiously. "Yeah. There's nothing like New York in the spring. The shows are great, the restaurants are superb. They rival Paris or Rome. The city buzzes with more energy than firecrackers and some of the biggest deals going down. The city never sleeps. It's pure, unadulterated excitement."

"Oh, now you're teasing." She relaxed. "Well, I'm sure those cities are all you've said, but I'm glad you could make New Beginnings tonight, at any rate. I merely have my fifth-graders to excite me tomorrow. Then Saturday...I guess I'll do some shopping."

"Buy something new." He let his glance slide over her full figure. She seemed slimmer than when he was last in town. She'd put some style in her hair, too. "Something bright pink."

She laughed. "I haven't worn pink since I was in grammar school. I don't think of pink as being a color for grown-ups."

"Why not? That's nonsense. I think you'll look very pretty in pink. Bright pink."

Bright pink?

She swallowed. "Okay. I'll see what I can find."

He gave a sharp nod. "You do that. And do me a favor, will you? Tell Pastor Mike that...hmm, that I'll see him in about two weeks. Now I really do have to go." He touched her shoulder again, this time meaning it as more than a contact point. "You've been a bright spot in my evening, Cassie. See you in two weeks."

Cassie watched him stride out of the room, her heart beating faster. In the space of thirty minutes, he'd gone from somber to playful. What was up with him?

But she'd been a bright spot for him? She could positively swoon at the thought. If it were real…

She'd pretend it was. What was the harm? She could tell her school friends at lunch.

Yet as she drove home, she wondered where Peter lived. He'd never mentioned his neighborhood, never talked of his friends. Or family. She hadn't seen his motorcycle in the lot, but then she hadn't been outside to look for it while Peter was here.

The fact that he showed up on Thursday evenings to New Beginnings indicated that he lived nearby. But then why didn't he come every week? And except for Easter Sunday, why hadn't he ever come to church on Sundays?

Never mind. All she knew was that she had to buy something pink. She'd wear it in two weeks and hope he'd notice. And she'd get her hair done again, too.

Cassie counted the days, never mentioning Peter to anyone at lunch. She baked cookies for Donna's birthday, but didn't eat any. She hadn't been eating as much since she was living alone and not cooking full meals. She simply didn't see the need to bother. She cleaned the house on Saturday, and as she looked the rooms over critically she saw they needed some updating. She'd lived with it so long, she simply didn't notice. The house was decorated in the style from thirty years ago.

But an update cost money, and they'd had to replace the furnace the last year her father was alive. She bit her lip. She'd have to tackle it this summer, she decided. At least some paint, she mused. Something brighter. When she had more free time.

She was excited to attend church, both on Thursday nights and Sunday mornings. It was livelier than her father's church. Peter wasn't there, but she liked Pastor Mike's short sermons on Thursday nights, and the more formal ones that Pastor Hostetter gave on Sundays. Pam Lawson usually came, and she sat next to her.

"Are you free next Saturday?" she asked after Sunday's service.

"Hmm, my oldest son is busy in college, my youngest has…something or other," Pam answered. "I suppose I could be. Why?"

"Can you go shopping with me?" Cassie asked tentatively. She hadn't made plans with anyone outside of New Beginnings meetings, except for Easter Sunday, and she didn't know if her new friendship would take. "I need some new clothes and I'm afraid I'll choose something awful. All those bright colors are for younger people. Know what I mean?"

Pam's glance was one of surprise. "Sure. But I don't think we're too far gone for bright colors yet. In fact, I think you'd look great in them."

"Really?" Cassie's heart swelled with delight. A real friend at last.

"Yes. Besides, I could stand to go on a little shopping spree. Both boys need new jeans and pants."

"Well, I mean to find something pink. And you should look for something new for you, too. No boy's clothing. Only women's things."

Pam tipped her head at Cassie, squinting her eyes in recognition. She grinned. "Okay, you're on."

"Hey, I'll go. I don't have anything better to do," spoke up Maggie Wegland, a newcomer to New Beginnings. "My children are all on their own these days. They're all in college. I can't count on seeing any of them unless one of them needs money or something."

"Great! A real girls' day out. Where can we meet?" Cassie asked, her glance going from one woman to the other.

They settled on a time and place to meet in the Independence Mall. Saturday promised to be a big day for Cassie. It had been a long time since she'd had quality time with friends of her own age. No one at work really qualified. She couldn't even remember the last time she'd shopped with friends. And new friends from New Beginnings definitely was worth her time.

On Saturday, the three women laughed and giggled all day. The surprising thing came when Cassie tried on a pair of dark pants. They were too big.

"I guess these are cut differently than my usual brand," she told Pam.

"No," said Maggie, looking at the slacks. "These run true to size. Maybe you've lost weight."

"I never thought of that," Cassie replied. She mused on her clothes. True, they fit easily…more comfortably. But then she was used to baggy clothes.

But not *that* baggy.

"Well, what do you know? I have!" Cassie exclaimed. "Imagine that!"

Pam looked her over. "Yes, you have. You've been attending New Beginnings for what? Three months or more? I think you're slimmer now than when you began."

"Do you think this thing would be, um, too tight?" She picked up a T-shirt and another pair of black slacks, a size smaller.

She'd be mortified if the slacks were too tight. Her dad's critical voice would haunt her. Wearing anything tight was for teens, in his opinion, and all teens dressed scandalously these days, he used to say. She'd worn baggy clothing for as long as she could remember.

"Maybe. But I'd get it anyway," said Maggie. "*You* can't be called Saggy Maggie."

"Saggy Maggie?"

"Yeah. You haven't sagged like I have. You know…with three pregnancies and three children? And age…."

Cassie giggled, mirth in her gaze. Then Pam gave an answering chuckle. Maggie doubled over in laughter. They drew glances from other customers, but Cassie couldn't have cared less. Her father wasn't here to scold and frown. He wasn't here to be scandalized by their down-to-earth, honest talk.

Cassie went home that night with laughter still in her system, and the empty house wasn't quite so silent.

Next Thursday, two new people came to the New Beginnings meeting, but

Peter wasn't there. Cassie stoically accepted the fact that perhaps Peter would never return. He had to work, he'd said. But what did he do for a living?

It didn't matter. Cassie was gaining confidence through her involvement in New Beginnings. Being alone no longer felt new or scared her out of her comfort zone. Since her father's passing, she was free to indulge her imagination as often as she chose. That was one of the main reasons she'd joined New Beginnings— to find a new life, to create something for herself beyond what she'd known. She was tired of imagining drifting into old age alone, filling her life with favorite television programs or crossword puzzles, with no one to talk to or celebrate life's little pleasures.

So what if Peter really didn't return? She was blessed enough by his attention, and she didn't expect more.

But Peter did return. Cassie's heart

leaped high when she spotted him coming through the door at a New Beginnings meeting, on time even. He paused in the doorway to gaze about the room. The day had been warmer, and he looked tanned, his silver hair brushed back neatly, wearing a bright-blue T-shirt that matched his eyes.

Cassie was on her way to sit down. She slowed, watching him. She wondered if he had dressed to seem more casual, as the others did. The crowd wore jeans and T-shirts now that the days were warmer.

His gaze stopped, arrested by someone on the other side of the room, and his expression changed somehow. Cassie didn't know who he was looking at; she couldn't take her eyes off Peter. Then he quickly entered the room, his eyes flashing and, spotting Cassie, came her way.

"Hi, Peter." She scooted into a row of chairs. She hoped she didn't sound too eager to see him. "Um, you're just in time. Pastor Mike is about to start the program."

"Sorry if I'm late. Couldn't get away before now."

"You're not late. Just on time."

After the opening prayer, Pastor Mike had something new for them, a get-acquainted exercise. "We've been studying the life of Jesus up till now. But we don't know enough about each other, and I think it's time we did. After all, how can we minister to each other when we know nothing about our neighbor?

"Let's divide into groups," Pastor Mike said, looking around. "No more than six in a group, and I want you to talk about your childhood. Choose three points. Talk about where you lived, who your best friend was at age seven, and what your favorite thing to eat was on Sundays. I'll give you thirty or forty minutes. Then we'll come back together in a large group and see how it worked."

Cassie scooted her chair back and looked to where Peter would sit. The room clamored with noise as chairs screeched along the floor, making small circles. Cassie, Peter and two other people Cassie barely knew, Elizabeth Johnson and Shelley Burgess, came together. Then Charlie and Linda joined them.

She glanced over at Pam, in the next circle. Her friend gave an encouraging smile, then her attention went to her own circle. Maggie was on the other side of the room.

No one said anything at first. Cassie, used to taking charge in a classroom, stiffened her spine. She supposed it was up to her.

"Okay. Who's going to start?" Cassie asked, glancing at each of her circle mates.

"I will," said Elizabeth. "Let's see…I grew up in an apartment in the center of Kansas City—"

"May I sit in here with you?" Lori interrupted. "The other circles are all set."

So was theirs, Cassie thought. But as the murmurs of "Sure, scoot in" and "Nice to have you" were given, she shoved back her chair to create room for a seventh member.

Lori set her chair close to Peter. She smiled sweetly at him, her brown eyes soft, before glancing at the others.

Cassie hadn't taught school all these years without recognizing all the signs of pirating away a friendship.

"All right," she said in her no-nonsense teacher's voice. "Let's start again. Elizabeth, you were saying?"

Then she was lost in Elizabeth's story. Cassie found the accounts much more interesting than she'd thought she would. Elizabeth was a city child with one sister; Shelley a child of the suburbs, one of four children. Charlie had grown up on the East Coast, and was stranded here in the Midwest because of his two children and grandchildren.

When it was her turn, Cassie spoke of

the large, old-fashioned house she grew up in, the house with stiff rules, and the pot roast that was always served on Sundays because it was easy to put in an electric roaster while the family was at church.

"I had a school friend when I was seven, a girl named Becky. Becky had short black hair and was a whiz at the jungle gym, and I thought she was the greatest. I really admired her. But I was always so clumsy and tore half my clothes in trying to emulate her, that I was often in trouble because I didn't behave like a little lady."

She didn't reveal that she had never invited friends to her house to play. "They make too much fuss...." her mother had said. Or that Cassie seldom was allowed to go to a friend's house to play, either. Her parents didn't encourage the exchange, and as the years went on, she had ceased to ask.

Lori brushed her hair behind her ear

and smiled at them all, glancing at Peter. She had perfect teeth, Cassie thought.

Lori had grown up sharing a room with two sisters who fought over clothes, roller skates, hair barrettes, dolls and, later, boyfriends. She chuckled. "I never knew what we would eat on any given day. Mom always popped out a casserole or something."

Lucky Lori, Cassie mused.

Then it was Peter's turn. "I grew up in—" he stopped a moment to think "—a large house, I suppose you could say. Larger than most, I guess. And my mother died while I was quite young. She didn't cook much. I don't recall… hmm…we didn't go to church much, either. I guess I didn't have a spiritual education. That's why I like New Beginnings, I suppose."

He blinked in surprise, and glanced quickly over his shoulder to where Pastor Mike stood. Oddly, it was true— he liked the organization, and he liked

Pastor Mike. He had come to find his brother, but found that he actually enjoyed the spiritual teachings.

It was a surprise to him. He'd never imagined in a million years something so ordinary as a social organization based on Bible teachings could capture his interest.

He cleared his throat, and continued. "Um, my best friend when I was seven was Virgil. He taught me to play baseball. That's all."

He fell silent.

He didn't bother to say that Virgil was his father's personal assistant. Or that he'd lived through a series of stepmothers—four, to be exact. Or that he'd spent his grade school years in a military academy.

He didn't say he'd been a lonely little boy.

But if he'd been lonely as a child, he made up for it as an adult. When he finished college, he'd taken over the reigns of Tilford Real Estate like a race-horse let out of a chute. He worked hard, and played harder, seeking an antidote to those lonely childhood years. The restaurants and bars he'd mentioned in Paris and Rome were near his homes—in Paris and Rome. He visited each more than once a year.

He'd married twice, both women beautiful, blond, sleek and sophisticated, and one of them had given him his son, Danny.

He waited for a familiar pain to carve out a chunk of his heart. When it eased, he thought "never again" for the thousandth time and closed his mind with a sharp snap. He'd never marry again. Oh, he'd made sure his ex-wives had received plenty of alimony. They were content. But he wasn't going to make his father's mistakes with relationships.

No, he'd remain single. But it hurt badly to realize that the Tilford dynasty would die for lack of an heir.

He stared at his hands now. Self-consciously, he folded them. Idly, he wondered what made him self-conscious now…at this moment, when he'd never suffered from that particular peculiarity. Was it because no one here, in this out-of-the-way place, knew him? Knew he owned a billion-dollar business?

They'd recognize the Tilford name quick enough.

These people, all of them, were ordinary people. With ordinary jobs, everyday lives. No one asked him about those struggling years. No one mentioned marriages. Better to put them in the background.

He glanced up just as he mulled this over. And right into the eyes of someone he knew. Good grief! He hadn't seen Samantha Gray since that first meeting. What was Samantha Gray doing here? In Independence, Missouri?

Chapter Six

Peter leaned sideways behind Cassie just a bit to block Samantha's view of him. It was a good thing Samantha had her profile to him…but he didn't mistake it. He'd seen her too many times in the jet set in Europe. Had an occasional dinner with a group that included Samantha and her husband.

Yet it had been a long time ago. Hadn't her husband died a year or two ago?

Cassie gazed at him oddly, but he simply returned her gaze and smiled serenely.

He peeked again. Sure enough, it was

Samantha. What had he read in the European papers? A car crash…. But her husband, Count something or other, had died before, he thought. What was she doing here at New Beginnings?

He had to leave quickly, or the game was up.

But just then he spotted Eric, who'd walked in…what about him? He appeared flustered at seeing Peter, and hesitated to sit down.

Pastor Mike spoke, grabbing his concentration. "All right. Very good. You've made a start. Now I want you to get up from your seats and create new circles. Tell your circle mates the same three pieces of information."

"Oh, that's not fair," wailed Lori with a longing stare at Peter. "We were just becoming acquainted."

"Suits me," muttered Charlie.

"Ah, come on, Lori," said Elizabeth, leading the way toward another circle. "It'll be fun."

Cassie pasted a smile on, and scooted back her chair. "See you later, Peter."

Peter stood, paying Lori little mind. Lori fluttered her lashes, then took off herself, thank goodness. Cassie strolled toward another group without giving him a glance.

He immediately turned his back on Samantha. If she recognized him, then so be it. But he'd stay out of her way as long as possible. He watched as Eric reluctantly took a chair in the circle in the far corner of the room. Peter practically broke his neck getting there, dodging someone in his way, but he claimed the last chair.

Eric threw him a cold stare, then dropped his eyes. He leaned forward, his forearms on his knees, and looked at the floor.

"Quickly, people. Settle in and start the rounds," instructed Pastor Mike.

Peter glanced at Pastor Mike over his shoulder. Pastor Mike nodded slightly, letting him know he was aware of the situation. After the first meeting, the pastor had encouraged Peter not to give up on Eric. To persist in making contact.

He'd hoped for their family ties to connect. Peter felt more than hope. He longed for that very thing.

Chairs scooted together. This circle was only five people. Besides Peter and Eric, their group included Pam Lawson, Maggie Wegland and Beth Anne Hostetter, the pastor's wife.

Had Beth Anne sat in this circle to help them?

"Okay. I can begin," said Beth Anne. She had short hair that was going white and a wide mouth and she reminded Peter of Julia Roberts. "Let's see…. I lived on a small farm in southern Missouri. I had two older brothers who spoiled me." Her voice lowered with sudden sadness. "One was killed in a farm accident when I was a teen."

Sympathy from the circle came pouring out before Beth Anne finally said, "No, it's all a long time ago." She took a breath. "But my mother never quite got over it, and I turned to the Lord for comfort. He has never failed me." She gave Peter a knowing glance. "But oh, the dinners we had. Fresh vegetables and fruits in the summer, canned ones in the winter. There isn't a need now to can— we put a lot in the freezer. I guess my best friend was Millie, the girl down the road. She was a year older than I, and she had a crush on my other brother, Sam. Okay, now it's someone else's turn."

Peter was next. He related the same facts as he had in the first circle, but this time he spoke of having four stepmothers. He spoke slowly, wanting to say so much more, to tell Eric of his early life, to impart his sorrow that they'd lost each other over the years. "My four stepmothers all came and went quickly, it seemed. I scarcely recall their names. Except one, whose name was Faye."

Eric made not so much as a flicker when Peter mentioned Eric's mother. "She had pretty dark eyes. I think my father really loved her…in his way."

"What happened?" asked Beth Anne.

"Well, I was in military school most of the time, then college, so I don't know what happened." His voice grew husky. "My father refused to talk about it. She just disappeared with her little boy and I never saw them again."

He was silent a moment, watching Eric intensely, then added as an afterthought, "I don't remember what we ate on Sundays."

Peter thought Eric would bolt before it was his turn to talk. He remained still while Peter talked, only his fingers pushing together, up and down, up and down, showing his discomfort. But when it came to his turn, he glanced briefly up, anywhere but at Peter, then one brief glance directly into Peter's eyes. His gaze, flashing anguish and anger and hurt, hit Peter like a hammer.

"I grew up in foster families," Eric began on a husky note. He cleared his throat, and his voice grew stronger. "Two were actually all right. They treated us kids fairly and we had enough to eat. On Sundays, I got to help fix the meals. There were eight boys, so we fought a lot...

"My favorite playmate...was a—a brother, I guess, who gave me piggyback rides. I was little then, so I don't recall his name."

Peter felt like he'd been hit in the middle with a hard-thrown baseball. Look up, please...aw, please, Eric...just once, just to see the look in your eyes...don't you know that was me? That I was the one who gave you piggyback rides?

Someone else spoke, but Peter couldn't follow the woman's story. A rush of elation filled him. He'd gotten through…Eric had actually listened. He knew something of what Peter had gone through. And he knew something of Eric's story….

It grieved him, suddenly. Tore his heart into shreds.

Yet Eric wasn't ready to be friends.

Pastor Mike called them to assemble once more, and Peter eagerly rose, only to have Eric turn his back and disappear out the door. But somehow Peter didn't think it was forever. He'd made contact, honest contact, and now Eric knew Peter was his brother.

He'd wait. What did he have to lose? Then he realized he should tackle talking to Samantha, the sooner, the better.

As soon as the meeting ended in prayer, he rose and found Samantha, who was sitting with a friend.

"Can I talk to you?"

She turned, showing the long ugly

scar down her cheek. It drew up her skin around it, stretching to affect the corner of her mouth a bit. Shocked, Peter quickly hid his reaction while her eyes reached up to his face in surprise.

"Well, of all people! Peter—"

He held his curiosity in a tight check, and let no emotion at seeing her face show on his. Samantha's beauty had been known worldwide; that car accident was more tragic than he'd realized.

"Sorry." He flashed an apologetic glance at her seatmate at his interruption. "I need to talk to you. Is now a good time?"

"Why, of course, Peter." Samantha turned to Karen, asking, "I'd love some coffee, Karen. No cookies, if you don't mind. Will you get them?"

"Sure." Karen glanced knowingly at Peter, then left them.

Peter sank to the empty chair beside her, and murmured, "I heard about your accident. I'm so sorry."

She sucked in her lips before she spoke. "Thanks, Peter. I still have some surgeries to undergo. But what in heaven's name are you doing in Independence?"

"Taking care of business, what else? But…I, um, I'm known here as Peter Scott. None of these people know about me except Pastor Mike, and I'd like to keep it that way."

"Ah. I understand. You don't want me to give you away."

"That's it." He raised his eyebrows, and thought to add, "Please?"

"All right. I won't say anything."

"Thanks. Now, how are you getting along? Where are you staying?"

"I'm getting along…all right, I suppose. I'm at my mother's house. She lives nearby."

"Hmm, I never knew where you were from. Heard from Nicholas?" He mentioned her European brother-in-law.

"Not so you'd notice." She shrugged

and frowned. "I don't hang out with the crowd that parties anymore. They, ah, don't interest me any longer."

"I see. Well, you're in good hands here. Pastor Mike has some good teachings."

"Yes…well, Biblical teachings are universal, aren't they?"

Or very personal, Peter thought. Then he was surprised at his thought. Pastor Mike was teaching him more about spiritual matters than he thought possible for him to learn. More about The Man who had lived and died and risen again two thousand years ago.

Did he believe that? He didn't know, but he was gaining an intense interest in the Jesus stories. When Pastor Mike talked of Him, it touched a place deep inside him.

Peter noticed Samantha's friend approaching.

"Yes. Um, here comes your coffee. I must be going. But remember your promise? For now, anyway."

"Yes, I will."

Peter gazed about the room as he walked toward the door. He thought Samantha would keep his secret. Normally, he didn't care, but it would only complicate matters for the moment.

His real concern now was Eric. He hoped Eric would put the pieces together. He wondered if he should pursue the man. His home was nearby in a set of apartments, about fifteen minutes away. Pastor Mike had told him so, confirming the report he'd received from his private investigator. He'd driven by the building the last time he'd been in town.

He'd been tempted to see if Eric was home….

But Peter wasn't ready to risk it…yet.

What was he going to do? The matter was taking far longer than he had anticipated, but he hadn't imagined his brother didn't remember him. Irritation needled him. Eric wasn't ready to admit he needed his brother.

Yet Peter did. He was honest with himself. He'd wasted long years in not caring. He regretted those years now. He needed someone who was from his own family.

He looked around for Cassie to say good-night. She somehow had a soothing effect on him, and he felt talking to her a few moments would settle his emotions.

She and Pam Lawson were busily passing out coffee. He spied a plate of cookies, and grabbed one. "Hmm…these are really good. Who baked them?"

"Oh, Pam did," Cassie said with a smile. Her eyes appeared soft and sympathetic. She had little dents at the edges of her smile that intrigued him. "She's our champion baker."

"Say, Cassie, I skipped dinner. In fact, I haven't eaten since a late breakfast. Want to go get a bite to eat?"

"All right." She sounded surprised. "I know a place we can go."

"Okay. Let me speak to Pastor Mike, then we'll leave. Oh, um…I left my car…I had someone drop me off. Can we take yours?"

"Sure, but where's your bike?"

"It blew a gasket." She wouldn't know the difference, and didn't bat an eye. "You get your car and I'll be right out, okay?"

Cassie watched him go, then turned to Pam as Lori walked up. "Well, it looks like I have a date. See you all next week," she blew over her shoulder. Pam grinned, but she didn't wait to see Lori's reaction.

They drove to the nearby main road and found a drive-in. Peter ordered the works—a huge hamburger, fries and Coke. Cassie ordered a vanilla shake. There were tables outside, where they sat in the fresh air. Cassie hugged her sweater against the cool spring breeze.

"That was quite an exercise we had tonight," she said, watching Peter bite into his sandwich.

"Mmm…it sure was. I didn't know how much I *didn't* know about, um, everyone. Still, there's a lot to learn. For instance, you're an only child?"

"Uh-huh. I used to beg my mother for a baby brother or sister, but she always said it was too much bother and mess. I was born late into their marriage, you see, and…and I guess raising me was too much of a strain for her and my father."

He gave her a skeptical stare. "Were you a wild child?"

"No, not at all. I was the princess on display. My parents liked to show me off, but they always expected perfect behavior."

"Something you said gave me the idea they were rather strict."

"They certainly were. I had to abide by strict rules," she said, smiling. "And you went to military school? How was that?"

He chuckled. "Also strict. I guess I

made my share of trouble. Nothing serious, though. I wanted my father's approval too much."

"Did you get it?"

"Not really. Say, this hamburger is the best I've tasted in a long while. I'm almost tempted to order another."

She laughed at his delight. "Well, it's your call."

"Nah. I'll be satisfied with this. If I eat too much I'll gain weight. And I won't sleep tonight."

She dropped her eyes and poked her straw at her shake. She thought of all the times she'd taken second helpings under her mother's urging, and how her father had always called her his "little fat hen."

Peter leaned back and stretched. "Cassie, do you know anything about the real estate in this town?"

He sure had mastered the art of changing the subject, Cassie thought. He did it with such ease.

"Not really. Why do you ask?"

"I'm thinking I might buy a…um, town house or something. For when I'm in town. Staying at the hotels is becoming a grind."

"In Independence?" Her voice was incredulous.

"Yeah." He raised an eyebrow. "What's wrong with Independence? It's the Harry Truman town, isn't it?"

"B-but you'd have to have something to put down." She picked up their trash and looked about for a trash bin. Her curiosity heightened. "Um, I mean…do you have enough? Income, I mean? To make payments and all that?"

He rose from the picnic table. It was hard to keep his laughter down, she was so ignorant of his wealth. "What makes you think I can't buy something so simple?"

"Well, I assumed, I guess." She opened the car door, then slid into her seat. "I'm sorry, but I thought…never mind. I guess I was wrong."

"Want to go with me to look?" He ignored her misunderstanding. In fact, he'd encourage it. Better that she believe he didn't have much money. Besides, it tickled him to have her think it. He'd never been in the shoes of an ordinary man before. "You know your way around the streets, know the best places to see. We could see three or four on Saturday, couldn't we?"

"Yes, of course. All right." She turned the key. She'd have to look in the paper for ads. She'd seen a few listed around the town, but she had no idea if any were suitable. "I'd love to go. But wouldn't you rather settle on the Kansas side of town with the other yuppies?"

"What makes you think I'd like that? No, I'd prefer settling in this section of town."

"All right, then. Now, where to?"

He named a motel out near I-70. She blinked her surprise. It was a much better place than she'd suspected.

She pulled up to the entrance.

"Just a minute," he said, and glanced toward the glassed-in front lobby. He got out of the car. Coming around to the driver's side, he leaned in to say goodnight.

"I never told you how pretty you look in your pink T-shirt. You look great! And the color suits you."

"I do? It does?" Flustered at his compliment, her hands tightened on the steering wheel.

"Yeah. You thought I hadn't noticed, didn't you?"

"Well, I…sort of."

"Sorry I didn't say anything earlier, Cassie. Got a lot on my mind. I'll call you about Saturday."

He leaned in to kiss her, letting his lips touch hers. Her lips were softer than any he'd felt, and she leaned in to kiss him back. He suddenly felt connected, and didn't want to let her go.

He deepened the contact, his hand

going to cup her warm cheek. Why had he thought only to kiss her through a car window?

Her skin felt like velvet. She felt warm and vital, soft and…sweet.

When she pulled back, he let go slowly. He gazed at her, his eyes telling her how he felt.

Her eyes had grown huge. Luminous.

"Come in with me," he murmured. He wanted to be close with her, more than any woman he'd ever known.

A rare sadness crept into her face. She slowly shook her head. "I can't…."

"You can't? Why not?"

"I want to…but God's word says it's wrong. I—I don't do that sort of thing."

He pushed away, his throat tight. "It's all right. I'm sorry. I guess I got carried away. Don't worry about it. Good night, Cassie."

She gunned the motor, zipping out of the hotel parking lot like a fully throttled motorbike. Walking slowly, he entered the motel, thinking of her. She was a good woman, a Christian woman, in every sense of the word. The more he thought about it, the more he realized she was right to tell him no. They hardly knew each other.

About to open his door, he paused with the key in his hand. She was a rare woman, indeed. And Peter found himself looking forward to seeing her again.

Chapter Seven

Cassie didn't know how she got home. She must have driven home on autopilot. Her mind replayed the kiss over and over. He'd kissed her. Kissed her! She wished she could experience it all over again.

Cassie's feet hadn't touched the ground since Peter walked away from her. She hadn't experienced that feeling since Tommy from down the street had kissed her. She'd been fourteen. Her father had caught them, and thereafter, she was barely allowed out of the house.

I'm living a new kind of life now…and I'll dream if I want to….

She went into the house in such a dreamy state, she left her mail in the mailbox on the front porch, put her car keys down on the kitchen counter instead of the hook by the back door as her father had always insisted, and kept floating.

She felt like listening to music. She put on an old record—she didn't own any of the latest electronic equipment— a recording of waltzes. That was one thing she'd buy when she had the extra money—a DVD player, and a stereo system. But when the notes filled the air, she merely stood in the middle of the floor and took them in, accepting the beauty of the music as something necessary to her mind and emotions.

She didn't know how she was going to sleep, or teach tomorrow. But when the record ended, she sighed deeply, and climbed the stairs to bed. Dreams were lovely…but reality always came crashing down. She had a test for the kids tomorrow, and three loads of laundry to do tomorrow night, and Saturday grocery shopping.

She climbed into the bed she'd occupied all her life, longing for something she'd never had. Was Peter really only a dream? Would he disappear in time? She didn't know, couldn't even guess. But she would enjoy his company as long as she could.

And in the end, she said not a word at lunch to her teacher friends. Her feelings were too precious to share.

On Saturday she was up early, rushing to do a bit of housework. She began listening for the phone at seven, knowing it was too early for Peter to call. When he finally called at a little after eight, she was ready.

Though she wouldn't tell him that.

"Cassie, I'm going to line up some houses to see today. Do you think five or six will be too many? Can we start at nine o'clock?"

"My, you are eager. What makes you think I can be ready in—" she looked at her watch "—thirty-eight minutes?"

She could positively see his enticing grin, conveyed through the telephone line. "Thirty-eight minutes, huh? Just enough time for me to make three more calls. You'll be ready. See you then."

Three more calls? On a Saturday morning?

At a minute before nine she heard the roar of his motorcycle. So…it had been repaired, had it? And he expected her to drive, did he?

She met him on her front porch wearing a new print dress. In pink. Because it was flattering, she thought, and that was part of her new life.

She expected him to compliment her on it. Instead, the first thing he said was, "You'll have to change."

"What?" She blinked her surprise.

"Um, sorry. But you can't wear that dress—pretty as it is." He looked at her as he took off his helmet. "Haven't you got some jeans? And you'll need something different than that sweater."

"Well, yes, I have them, but they're kinda, um, disreputable."

"Doesn't matter," he said as he pulled out a second, brand-new helmet. "Disreputable is in, didn't you know? Put 'em on. You'll need to hurry, though. Bought a new helmet for you. Our first appointment is at nine-thirty."

She stared at the extra helmet. They were to travel on the motorcycle? "You must be kidding!"

"Not a bit. Now get going."

She whirled on her pink high heels and ran up her steps into the house and up the stairs. She left the front door open. Digging into the bottom of her chest, she found her jeans, worn and patched on one thigh, that she wore to tend to the roses. Hurriedly, she threw her dress and matching sweater on the bed and slipped into the jeans. Then she chose her brand-new pink T-shirt to top it.

But she had only her cardigan sweater to top it, and he'd said not to wear it. What did she have that would do? She had an old raincoat…but that would be too long. Well, she'd just make do with the sweater.

When she tripped downstairs, she found Peter in her living room, looking at the cover of the album she had played. He glanced up, taking in her jeans and sneakers.

He handed her the mail from yesterday while inspecting her from top to toe. "Your mailman comes early."

"Actually, that's yesterday's mail. He usually comes later in the day." She laid the mail on the coffee table, not even looking through it.

"That's better." He nodded. He held something in his left hand, and now handed it to her. "But you'd better wear this, I think."

He handed her a black leather jacket.

"All right," she said, thinking it was his. Yet he still had his on. Had he borrowed this one?

But when she slipped her arms through, the sleeve length was just right. It fit around her body with a perfect fit. It dawned on her—this was a women's jacket, and it was new.

Her mouth fell open as she glanced up at him.

"This is new…."

"Yes, it is. Now can we go? We're going to be late."

"But did you buy this? I mean…"

"Let's talk about it on the way." He took her arm and headed out of the door.

"But Peter," she protested. "Wait a minute." She turned her back to lock the door while he continued on to the bike.

When she approached the bike, he handed her the helmet to put on. Her stomach quaked with nerves, but she'd be strung up by her thumbs before she'd refuse to ride after all the preparation he'd made. Or succumb to her own nerves.

Climbing on behind him, she bit her lip. In for a penny, in for a pound, she thought, as her mother would say. She took a deep breath and slipped her arms about his middle, her heart in her throat. A moment later, they were roaring down the street.

Her next-door neighbor, Mrs. Warren, who was out watering her tulips, waved at her.

Cassie waved back with high abandon.

"Which way is Albon Street?" shouted Peter.

She tried to snuggle close to him, but the helmets bumped. She contented herself with a shouted back, "Left."

They slowed on the proper street. Three rebuilt buildings sat in the midst of older apartment buildings. A huge sign announced they were now leasing.

The real estate woman met them at

the door. She showed them around, then showed them a map of the different apartment layouts.

"The kitchen is a bit small," Cassie whispered.

"That's because you're used to your kitchen, which is rather large," he returned.

"Now this looks out over the pool, and you can go right out of your living room to it," said the woman.

Cassie ducked her head and bit her lip. Peter picked up on her dislike.

"Thank you," Peter said, honesty in his voice. "I appreciate your showing us around, but I have a couple of others I'm looking at. I'll let you know by next week."

As they got on the bike, Peter asked, "What's the matter, Cassie? Don't you like to swim?"

"Yeah, but a pool located immediately at the rear of your apartment isn't good. You'd get all the noise."

"Good point. Now where is Ginger Street? How far and which way?"

She gave him precise directions, and they were off. They visited three apartments by one o'clock, Peter asking opinions and Cassie commenting, then stopped for lunch. Peter pulled into the parking lot of a nice restaurant along Thirty-Ninth Street. Cassie was ever so glad. She'd never thought looking at apartments was so hard.

"Let's rest and have lunch," Peter said. He turned off the bike and let Cassie climb off first.

"Fine by me." She shook her head, glad to be free of the helmet. She finger-combed her hair, wondering how messy it was. But it fell about her ears, and Peter's gaze told her it wasn't too bad. "I think we're seen too much. I don't remember if apartment B over on Crisp Road has all the kitchen appliances included, including a nice trash compactor, or was it that town house on Ginger Street?"

They entered the restaurant, and waited to be seated.

He chuckled. "I think it was on Ginger Street."

"Well, the price was out of sight, and the entry will be hard to get out of during rush hour," she whispered. "How many of these do we have to look at today?"

The hostess led them to a table then, so he delayed his answer.

"Only two more," he answered, sliding into his seat. "Aren't you having a good time? Can you take it?"

Opening up her menu, she hid behind it. "I suppose so. You should see what I have to put up with teaching school."

She didn't sound too enthusiastic. But Peter had said he needed a place to call his own, and they were going to hunt until he found one.

It wasn't so much that everything she saw was new, but it reminded her that in her house, everything was old—every stick of her furniture was faded and worn. Her father hadn't let her update a single item, and the furniture was scratched by his wheelchair. She'd lived with it so long she hadn't realized how drab and rundown the house had become. Until today. And she didn't have enough money to buy new or have painters come in unless she spent the small legacy from her aunt Susan.

It depressed her to realize what her summer project would be. Of all years, she'd wanted this summer to be free from worries. She'd hoped to hike around the city, thoroughly explore the Nelson Art Gallery, and walk a bit of the Katy Trail. She couldn't afford a real vacation, but getting out and about in the city would suit her.

Now she'd have the house to consider.

Suddenly, he declared, "I'm kind of tired of looking at apartments. Let's concentrate on town houses."

She peeked at him over the menu. "Peter... can you really afford a town house? I mean… you seem to be gone a lot. An apartment would take less up-keep."

"That's true. But I'm tired of hotels. And I can see…that is, I'll be coming back here for most of a year, whenever I can. It would pay off in the long run if I simply had a place to crash when I'm here."

"Um, okay. But houses require a lot of upkeep, you know. Even town houses. You'll have to spend time on whatever you buy. Are you willing to do that?"

"Yeah, I know all that," he said, grinning with a glint in his eye. "But I can pay for services."

The waitress took their order, then later set two plates of barbecue before them and refilled their glasses of iced tea.

"Can you? Really?" she asked as soon as the waitress had gone. She wondered again what he did for a living. She hadn't asked him—but he looked fit enough.

In fact, he looked as though he might work out. But he always seemed in a hurry.

"This is good barbeque." He changed the subject again. "Say, let's skip looking any more today. Let's go to a movie instead."

"This afternoon? All the movies will be filled with teenagers and families."

"Aw, come on, Cassie. How long has it been since you've been to an afternoon movie?"

She couldn't recall, it had been so long. "All right, you've convinced me. I haven't seen a movie in ages."

"I'll find out the movie times," he said, and pulled out his cell phone.

They finished their lunch, then drove to the movie multiplex. They picked a comedy and laughed till tears ran down their cheeks. When it was over, they strolled out into the late afternoon, hand in hand. It was starting to rain.

"Ooh, it wasn't supposed to do this till

midnight," she commented, quickly putting on her helmet.

"That's one problem I haven't figured out yet." Peter smiled. "How to control the weather."

"I suppose you should take me home. We'll be wet through by the time we get there."

"It's been a great day, hasn't it?" Peter said as he climbed on the bike. He thought of all the work he'd neglected in order to take this day off. He'd probably work far into the night. But the impulse to spend it with Cassie had been right. He felt more relaxed than he had for years.

"It certainly has. Are you going to church tomorrow? Pastor Mike is doing the preaching. Beth Anne told me Thursday night that they'll be out of town."

"I didn't know that." He'd planned to fly home at first light tomorrow.

But there was a strong chance for him to see Eric tomorrow and, above all things, he wanted that. He wouldn't mind listening to Pastor Mike preach a whole sermon, either. The man was impressive, better than any of the men on his staff at getting to a point.

"I suppose I will. When is the service?"

She told him just as he started the motor. They zipped back to the house in no time. She removed herself cautiously from the bike while he remained on, his feet flat on the ground.

"Do you want to come in?" She sounded a little uncertain.

He glanced at her, a slow half smile spreading.

She hesitated, not mistaking the meaning of his smile. "T-to watch television."

His grin dissolved into a wry chuckle, and he kissed her tenderly. "No, thanks, Cassie. But I'll take a rain check, you can be sure."

Chapter Eight

Five phone calls waited for Peter when he entered his suite at the motel. He had left his business cell phone in the room. He let out a gusty sigh. Two of them were urgent. This was his world and he fell into it with relief, inevitability, but with a bit of regret, too.

He slipped out of his jacket and threw it onto the couch. Then he picked up the phone and punched in the first number as he sank down to relax while he talked. He talked steadily for twenty minutes, then, ending that call, immediately called the next contact on his list.

Tony Swartz came in, nodded his hello and opened up the laptop computer sitting on the table. Tony knew what to do, and Peter let him work without his direction. Returning these phone calls was important. He couldn't ignore them forever. Leaving them for longer than a day might lose him too much business. Yet he'd stay in town one more day, he decided, and try one more time to connect with his brother.

That decision made, he showered, sent Tony out for Chinese food and dutifully worked until midnight. He slept soundly.

The next morning he rose, feeling lucky. And blessed.

Blessed? Where had that word come from? It stopped him for a moment as he got dressed. He supposed he'd heard it from Pastor Mike. But he'd heard it from Cassie, too. It seemed a natural part in her speech.

Now it was creeping into his.

He grinned unconsciously. Well…perhaps today he'd be blessed to talk to his brother. He'd arrive at church early, he thought.

He took his late-model car, and drove to the Blue River Valley Community Church. He parked alongside a dozen cars in the parking lot, then strolled inside. He hung about in the lobby, hands shoved into his pockets, watching everyone as they entered.

Eric came in a bit late, but he came. Peter's heart lifted at seeing him. Just as he was about to call to him, Cassie interrupted from the opposite side.

"Peter?"

His head whipped around, then he said hurriedly, "Yes? Oh, hi, Cassie."

"Were you waiting for me?" Her eyes sparkled, and her mouth held just a hint of a smile. She wore a simple black dress, which highlighted her blond hair.

She looked beautiful!

"No…." The answer slipped out before he had time to think. Disappointment flashed in her eyes as he glanced back around, watching where Eric went. "I wanted to talk with that...that fellow. Excuse me."

Abruptly, he turned to leave. He'd have to make it up to her later, Peter thought. But right now his mind was on Eric.

He practically ran down the aisle to catch his brother. He slipped into a pew next to Eric, with no more room left for anyone else. Eric glanced up, showing his surprise only by a compression of his mouth. A mouth shaped much like his own, Peter noticed for the first time.

Eric quickly gazed around him, but there was nowhere for him to move without a major disruption; three children sat on the other side of him, and he'd have to crawl over Peter to get out of the pew. He had to remain where he was. He scooted over an inch.

The opening of the service began, and they stood for the first praise song. It wasn't unlike their Thursday nights,

Peter noted, and he started to sing, his voice telling of his hope.

Eric stared straight ahead; he cleared his throat and sang in his rich baritone. When the scripture was announced, Peter reached into the rack in front of him and pulled out the standard Bible that was there. He fumbled through, looking for Matthew, glancing from the side of his gaze to Eric's Bible. Where was the scripture?

Eric had his own Bible, he noticed. A worn, large, red-letter-print, leather-bound edition. His brother must spend a lot of time studying. He'd found the place.

Silently, Peter vowed to study more of the Bible by his next visit. He'd be hanged if he'd look a fool twice.

As the worship service proceeded, he began to relax. He was here alongside Eric. And inside his empty void of a heart, a tiny bit of faith began to grow.

He was caught up in the message of

the day. Matthew was a cool dude, he thought. How did Jesus know all that stuff? Much of the traits He urged were traits of good business practices—kindness and compassion, thoughtfulness and generosity. Paying attention to family. That was an issue he'd have to give more thought to. Like his father, he'd been lax there. He pondered Jesus's words, impressed in spite of himself.

He'd practiced those things…all except attention to family. He'd been a lousy husband, the two times he'd been married. He'd been a thoughtless, careless father to his one son. His son had died knowing very little of his father.

Peter felt overwhelmed with that pain….

He was trying to correct that now. He wanted to know his brother, wanted it with all his heart.

When the service began its closing with all heads bowed and the pastor praying, he quietly reached into his pocket and pulled out a small pearl ring. He gently laid it in Eric's hand, slightly open.

Eric gave him a flickering glance as his hand closed over the ring. His mouth moved, then he stared at the ring. Yellow gold, it featured three small, shiny, first-class pearls. Around the pearls, tiny gold leaves highlighted the setting.

Peter waited. The prayer came to an end.

The bustle of dismissal started about them. Purses were slung over shoulders, books picked up, children gathered. The children next to Eric stumbled through the narrow space to get out, two adults followed, and the aisle became clogged with people, greeting, chatting, leaving.

Peter and Eric remained where they were.

"What am I supposed to do with this?" asked Eric, his voice husky with emotion.

"It's yours." Peter licked his dry lips, hoping against hope that after the last confrontation with Eric, he would accept it. "Faye left it."

Eric attempted to hand it back.

"No, no. Please." Peter never begged for anything, but he couldn't keep that tone from entering his voice now. He said as gently as he could manage, his own voice low, "It belongs to you. It's the only thing of value Faye left. I don't know how I came into possession of it, but I thought you might want it."

"Why?" His eyes still on the ring, Eric's voice was stilted against a painful emotion. "Why are you giving this to me?"

"Because we share a father."

Eric's gaze flew to Peter's face. His mouth went slack as though he couldn't quite believe what he was hearing. His stare was searching.

"A father? You and I? But that would mean…"

The sudden understanding caught Peter by total surprise. Lord, help him! *Eric hadn't known!* Hadn't ignored him just for spite. He simply hadn't known. Hadn't Eric understood the last two times they'd met?

"I'm your brother, Eric." Peter swallowed. "Did you think I bothered you simply for sport?"

"I thought you were one of Faye's boyfriends," Eric mumbled, shame mixing with embarrassment and confusion.

"You thought—?" How could he? Yet looking back over their past contacts, Peter suddenly could see how the mistake was made. "No, no. My mother was Eileen. She died when I was only seven. Your mother came later, but she...I think she suffered from depression. Did you know?"

"No," Eric answered slowly. "I never saw Faye after I was about five or six, I think. Off and on for about a year. But her life was...rough. Filled with men.

Sometimes she would make promises, then forget them as easily. It was better when I went to foster care."

"So we both suffered the lack of mothering." The statement was made as a hard fact. One more thing they shared.

But while Peter's adult life was filled with ease, what had Eric's been? How was he living now? The report from the private detective told him his brother was single and worked at a factory. That didn't add up to much of a life.

Sudden guilt crept into Peter's thinking. He'd been blessed with the fortune he'd inherited and always had every material thing he could possibly desire. Too much, in fact.

But Eric had money coming to him— didn't he know that?

"Yeah. Mothering," Eric murmured, surprise showing. He licked his lips, not knowing what to ask, what information to exchange. He stared at the ring as though it could take him back in time.

Peter raked his mind to recall shared times.

"I played with you when you were just a little boy, taking you on piggyback rides. You talked of it at New Beginnings during that exercise, didn't you? Once, especially. I was home during vacation. About fourteen, I believe. Don't you remember? You were…I guess you were about four."

Eric glanced up again, staring hard. "Yeah, I think I do, a bit."

"But I saw you only three or four times in my life after that. I was away at military school. When I got back, you were gone. You and Faye."

Eric nodded. "So you've said in…our exercises. In New Beginnings."

The auditorium had emptied. The last usher came down the aisle to see about them.

"And Dad wouldn't answer any questions I put to him, so I had nothing…I had no way of tracing you…. Look, we're going to have to talk," Peter said. "Can we go somewhere? I have snapshots. Pictures. Even one movie reel with you on it. I recall one Father's Day—"

"I have to have time," Eric interrupted, standing abruptly, his eyes wary. Hiding hurt and puzzlement, yet a thread of hope. "I can't just... I'll try to sort all this out, but I can't stay now."

"I guess that's best. We can talk later." This had all come suddenly for Eric. Peter bit down on an order, trying not to show his disappointment, wanting to command his brother to talk to him. Yet he held his tongue. He stood, as well, and turned to the usher. "We're leaving. Sorry to have delayed you."

"That's okay," the usher said. "I'm not in a hurry. Did you want to talk with the pastor?"

"No, thank you. Not now." Later, thought Peter. Perhaps he and Eric together.

They walked up the aisle, a foot of space between them.

"Will you promise to call me?" Peter asked as they reached the lobby. He fought the urge to reach out and take Eric's arm, to touch his brother. This was the first nonangry meeting he'd had with Eric. He feared if he let his brother go, he might never see him again.

The usher waited, and they stepped outside.

Peter pulled out his card, and handed it to Eric. "I don't want anything from you, I promise, only—" It wasn't a complete lie. "I just want to get to know my brother. Here's my private number. Call me. Please? You can reach me anytime, day or night. I hope—"

He wanted a relationship with his brother more than he was willing to admit. But he wouldn't get it by forcing Eric to talk.

His mouth twisted, then he said more slowly, "I hope you call me. We have much to talk about. At the very least, we have to talk about your inheritance."

Eric glanced at the card, then put it into his pocket. Silently, he slowly nodded, then ducked his head and moved swiftly away. Peter watched him go. He didn't understand the hollow sadness that stole over him.

He thought about his own son, Danny, who had died of leukemia only the year before. Like his father, he hadn't spent much time with his son, either, until the last illness. Or Danny's mother, Barbara, a stranger to Peter now, who seemed content with her life. She had remarried a few years ago.

He grieved now…grieved for all the time lost. Grieved for not knowing his son well. He had no one to blame but himself. But it was that grief that caused him to wake up and think about family. When he realized he didn't have anyone of his own.

No one.

Not a single soul who really cared whether he lived or died, or how he might spend his money. His friends didn't. Oh, his staff cared—in a professional way. But personally?

He doubted it.

He'd been well taught about neglect, he thought. He'd suffered through those stepmothers himself. Then his father had died, leaving him a small fortune in real estate. He'd taken that small fortune and built Tilford Enterprises, a world-class company. He was one of the richest men in the world.

Peter shook himself, and got into his car. If he didn't return to that world, his company wouldn't remain world-class. The company gave back exactly what he put into it, he reminded himself. Time to be on his way.

Cassie heard the doorbell late in the day. It was almost dark. She opened the door, seeing a young man with a delivery of long-stemmed red roses. Her gaze on the box, her breath caught.

"For me?" she questioned the young delivery man. He squinted his eyes through round glasses.

He glanced again at the address, and said, "Are you Cassandra Manning?"

"Yes."

Placing the box into her hands, he said, "Then they're yours."

She'd never received roses before. She turned back into the house, excited to receive roses from Peter, but still hurt over his snub at church. All through the service, she'd sat beside Pam and smothered her hurt feelings with silence.

Finding a vase, she opened the box with care, marveling at the deep red color of the flowers. She was aware of the note…but she saved that for reading later. At that moment she wanted to appreciate her roses without thinking of who had sent them.

She carried the vase into the living

room and set them on the mantel. Then she decided they'd look better on the dining room table. She stared at them at that location. They looked lovely there, but she spent hardly any time in the dining room. Finally, she settled for the coffee table in the living room, where she often curled up on the couch.

She sat there now, and at last pulled the note from its envelope. The signature was Peter's, all right. Only two short sentences apologized for his snub this morning.

"My deepest apologies, sweetheart. Next time."

Her heart began to pound. He'd called her "sweetheart." Did he mean that?

Whether he did or not, she'd enjoy the roses. She wouldn't read too much into the apology, she decided. She'd just enjoy the attention for what it was. And the lovely roses.

Another surprise came the next morning at school.

"Miss Manning, would you please come to the office?" an announcement came over the buzzer, just before noon.

Cassie glanced up. Her class was in the middle of a math lesson. She glanced about the room, and said, "William, would you please act as monitor, and everyone else, stay put. Do the exercises on page twenty-three. I'll be back as soon as I can."

Cassie rose from her desk, and brushed down her denim skirt. Could Mrs. Hagan, that too-involved mother, be calling again? The woman called more often than Cassie was comfortable with, but she usually saved the calls until the end of the day. She left her classroom and hurried down the long hall toward the office. She approached the front desk, her anxiety showing, she was sure.

"What is it, Terry?" she asked the secretary.

"A delivery came for you," Terry said,

her eyes sparkling. "A personal delivery. I thought you might want these right away to put them in water."

A personal delivery? She glanced at a smiling Terry as she accepted a florist's box. The principal watched from her doorway, and the part-time secretary was smiling.

She glanced back at the box. Enormous curiosity overtook her anxiety. She lifted the lid. This time it was pink roses, two dozen of them. Her mouth practically dropped to the floor as the blood rushed to her cheeks. She spotted the card, but refused to read it in front of all these people. "I—I will. Thank you."

She turned to leave, noticing several heads peeking from open classroom doors. Her chin lifted with pride.

But who'd sent them?

Peter, who else? It certainly couldn't have been anyone else. But twice in two days?

Chapter Nine

It was close enough to lunch time for Cassie to release the children. The excited, curious children lined up to file out of the room, watching as she placed one hand on the box, then hurried from the room. Two little girls lingered behind. Blond, sharp-nosed little Bethany stopped at the desk while Cassie began to look for a vase large enough, and Dana, taller with brown hair, stood, her hands on her hips with her pierced eyebrow raised.

"Miss Manning, aren't you going to open that box?" asked Dana, with all the curiosity a ten-year-old can have.

"Why, yes, of course I am, Dana." She gave a brief smile and lifted the long box top, revealing perfect pink rose buds that were about to open.

"Ooh, they're so pretty. Are those from your boyfriend?" asked Bethany, her blue eyes wide, as she reached to touch one.

"No, just a friend."

"Well, my sister says that nobody sends roses but a sweetheart," insisted Bethany.

Finding a vase in the upper cabinet, Cassie set it on her desk. She took the roses from their box one by one.

"She does, does she?" she answered, rather absently. "Maybe just this time?"

"Uh-uh…." Bethany shook her head.

"Did you have a fight?" asked Dana, almost accusingly.

"A fight? Certainly not." Most of these children knew far too much of grown-up emotions, Cassie thought. "Can't they just be from a friend?"

"Nope." Dana shook her head. "I think they're from your boyfriend. And either he's gonna propose or he's saying he's sorry about something. What's his name?"

Cassie glanced up. Dana's awareness shocked Cassie, but not for the first time. She thought the ten-year-old more knowledgeable than was good for her.

A sharp ring sounded in the hall, relieving Cassie of the need to answer. "There's the bell, girls. Better run along to lunch now."

"All right," said Bethany. "But those roses sure are pretty."

They had no sooner left, than Donna popped her head through the door. "I heard you got roses! Is it true?"

"Um, yes…. Peter sent them." She still had not touched the note, other than to whisk it from sight into her top drawer.

"They're beautiful. Are you going to lunch today?" Donna made a face. "Why is he sending them? Did you guys fight or something? Everyone will want to know…."

Why did everyone assume they'd fought?

"I'll be along in a minute. I just want to…um, I'll be right there. I'll bring the roses to the teachers' lounge for all to enjoy."

"Smart idea. See you."

Slowly she sat down again, then pulled Peter's note from her drawer to read. But all it said was, "Once more— sorry. See you soon."

Cassie sighed with frustration. Would Peter ever tell her what he was really feeling? And how could he afford three dozen roses, the pink ones today after the red ones last night?

Nevertheless, she lifted her head as she strode down the hall, a huge smile lighting up her face.

Two weeks later, when she arrived home from school, Peter lay on her front porch swing—asleep. She hurried up the steps, then, with one foot on the porch, she spotted him. Her heart quickened. She quietly laid her books down on the floor, and tiptoed forward. His lashes lay against his cheeks like dark smudges.

He lay with one foot on the floor, an old ratty pillow under his head. He wore a gray suit that highlighted his silver hair, and his shirt was unbuttoned at the neck. His dark red tie lay crumpled on his chest; his phone lay clutched near his tie.

Who was he expecting to hear from? What was so important?

Yet he still wore those old run-down shoes, she noticed. Though polished to a shine, they still showed the marks of hard wear. Three dozen roses he could send her, but he couldn't afford to buy new shoes?

She leaned toward him, her hands on her knees. Her hair swung forward, and she was suddenly very glad she'd had it cut and styled again only last week. Should she wake him?

She put out a hand, but before she could touch him, he muttered, "Don't creep up on me."

Cassie jumped a foot back and caught her breath. "What are you doing here?"

She glanced up the street at the cars parked there. Nothing seemed unusual. No strange cars. A tiny boy colored on the sidewalk with chalk, and she assumed Mrs. Longacre, from two doors down, was entertaining her grandson again.

"How did you get here?"

"Had a friend drop me off."

A friend, huh?

She watched him slowly sit up. "He had, um, errands to do so I told him to run along. Thought I could get a ride with you to New Beginnings tonight."

She felt a level of relief, but she wondered if all his friends were so accommodating. It seemed to her, other than his motorcycle, he always needed a ride from someone who had a car. And where was his motorcycle, anyway?

"Okay."

"You're late."

"Not unusually so." She felt the freedom to stay longer at work, now that she lived alone. She shrugged. "I had some paperwork to take care of and I didn't want to bring it home with me— it doesn't matter, does it? Are you hungry? I could fix us something."

She thought of what she could feed him. There wasn't much in her cupboards these days, and she hadn't fixed a real meal since her father died.

"Yeah, I'm starving. I didn't eat lunch. But why don't we grab a quick meal on the way?"

"You have a habit of doing that, don't you? Grabbing a meal? Okay. That would do, I suppose. I think I only have soup on hand. Come on in while I clean up a bit. I'm always a little grubby when I come home from school."

He rose rather wearily, Cassie thought. What had he been doing that was so wearying?

"Would you like some iced tea? I have some of that in the fridge."

"Yeah, thanks, I would."

She went into the kitchen and chose the good glasses, the light-blue ones that seldom were used since her mother's passing five years before. She rinsed them, then filled them with ice cubes and tea. When she returned, he was staring at the pictures on her mantel.

"Those are my mother and father," she said, referring to the young couple smiling from the gold frame. "When they married."

"Uh-huh. Is this you?" He picked up the photo of her twenty-one-year-old self. Her hair was a mousy brown, and she'd hidden her glasses in her pocket the day the photo was taken, much to her father's disgust. A smile lay on her face, yet it covered a rare pensive look. She hadn't noticed that particular look in the mirror for years…she'd only thought it normal at the time. Now she thought that even then, she'd longed for something else from life—something bigger, something more than the life she had.

She'd been the dutiful daughter, coming straight home after school to prepare meals and clean house. Her mother's arthritis made life miserable, and she took it out on Cassie, usually. Dating was discouraged at first, then out of the question. Oh, there were a few boys in high school and in college, but not many.

They disappeared after a few dates.

"Yes, it's me. Here's your tea. I'll just run up and clean up, if you don't mind."

She took the stairs at a fast run. She washed her face and hands, brushed her hair and changed her blouse to a bright-blue one. She stared at her image in the mirror. That would have to do.

When she came down again, Peter was using his phone. His back to her, his hand on his hip, pushing his suit coat aside, he spoke forcefully. "I want that deal, Nicky. If they're dragging their feet now it's because they think they can get more money. Well, the price is more than sufficient, and I won't put up with any more nonsense. If they don't want it by tomorrow at ten, then I'll walk."

She remained quiet, waiting while he listened to his caller. Her mouth opened slightly; she knew her eyes were as big as saucers.

"All right, then. Thursday next."

Peter snapped his phone closed, then angrily hurled it onto the sofa, watching it bounce once. He stood stiffly for a moment. When he turned abruptly, she stared at him.

"What was all that about?" she asked softly, her gaze questioning.

The muscles in his face softened. He put a hand to his face and rubbed his temple. "Nothing. I may have lost out on a good deal on…um, never mind. It's nothing to worry us. Let's go get dinner. I'll catch up with Nicky later."

He took her arm as they left the house. Cassie turned to make sure the door was locked, then led him to her old blue sedan.

About to get in, she suddenly turned. "Oh, you forgot your phone!"

"No, I didn't." He slid into the passenger seat. "I want some peace for a bit. I'll get it later."

Peter without his phone? "All right. Where to?"

"I don't care. Surprise me." Cassie drove for ten minutes, then pulled onto Noland Road, and a few moments later, into the small parking lot of a restaurant.

They waited their turn in the front lobby, then took seats quickly when shown to a table. After they ordered, Cassie lay her menu down and asked, "What's the matter, Peter?"

"Nothing, just business as usual. Frustrations are normal. Look, just leave it, okay? I don't want to discuss it." He shrugged. "So I've lost one."

She fingered her fork. His jaw was clamped. "But it upsets you. You're tighter than a drum. Why can't I help, if only to listen?"

"Look, Cassie, I will tell you about… something that's bothering me, but not now. It's just too complicated."

"Then why do you bother to come?"

Why did he bother? He glanced at her, her fingers shuffling the silverware about. He reached out to touch her, wanting to feel warmth, wanting to draw from her soul.

Her hand lay warm and sympathetic in his.

"Because you give me a sense of… calm, I'd guess you'd call it. A sort of serenity. New Beginnings does that, too. You give me space, you don't crowd me, and I find that I look forward to the peace you give me."

Peter couldn't remember a time when someone had had that effect on him.

Their meal came, and they dug into their food.

Halfway through, Cassie smiled at him. "I never thanked you for the roses. The pink ones made quite a stir at school with my students and the other teachers. I was never so popular before. Everyone's convinced you're a marvelous man who knows what a woman likes."

He laughed. "I owed you an apology."

"That you did," she acknowledged, picking up her purse and pulling out her wallet. "But you shouldn't spend so much money. Red roses on one day, then pink roses the next day must have cost you a fortune. Now let's settle our bill. I think we should go Dutch treat tonight, and come to an arrangement of each of us paying our own way."

"Absolutely not!"

She glanced up. "But if we're to keep

seeing each other, I think we should establish the rules—"

There was laughter in his eyes. "What makes you think I need help paying the bill?"

"Well, I—that is, your business seems to be, um, rather tenuous. I, um, I couldn't help but overhear some of your conversation, and you seemed so upset."

He threw back his head and laughed. "Come on, Cassie, let's get out of here. There's nothing wrong with my business. I, um, can play when I want to."

Mumbling to herself, she followed him to the counter. He could play when he wanted to? What did that mean? Was he laid off…out of work too often? It seemed to her his unpredictable appearances spoke of a spotty work record.

She glanced at her watch, startled at the time.

She stood impatiently by while he paid the bill, then they left the restaurant and slid into the car. She looked at her watch again. "We're cutting it close. We'll be more than late if we don't hurry."

"All right. So drive."

She turned over the motor. "I don't like being late. It shows disrespect for others."

"You're absolutely right." He buckled his seat belt. "That's a good business principle."

"But you were going to tell me—"

He sighed. "Let's leave the explanations for now, shall we? I will tell you what's bothering me…in fact, I *want* to tell you about it, when the time is right." He doubted she'd understand the intricacies of a real estate buyout. "But it'll take longer than twenty minutes."

"Okay, okay," she conceded. "Let's just go."

They were quiet on the drive and arrived at New Beginnings just as Pastor Mike was about to speak. Quietly, they took seats in the last row.

Pastor Mike stood looking at the audience for a moment. "It's good to see you tonight. So many of you. Almost—" he counted quickly "—forty, now that Cassie and Peter have come in."

There were a few chuckles and turns of heads to glance their way. Cassie felt like squirming as one of her fifth-graders would, she was so embarrassed. She felt the heat climb her cheeks.

"Forty people searching for a new beginning, to start over in life." He looked down at the podium a moment, then at them again. "Me, too. But I'm telling you that it's all been decided, and it's you who has to find your own new beginning. It's you who has to discover God's love for you. Do you even *know* His enormous love? Do you?

"Do you know who you are? From the beginning of time you were created to love God…and to receive His love. Look for His favor at every point, in the small things as well as the large things in your life. Guidance sometimes comes from the most unexpected sources. I was reminded about something by our teens the other day. You…*we* are His children. And since He is a King, what does that make us? The King's kids.

"If you're having trouble making decisions in your life, think about this. He likes to give us gifts. But those gifts aren't always the ones we'd like, or easy ones. Sometimes they bring pain in order to bring growth."

Pastor Mike paused and stared at them again. "Listen for His direction. It will come. Now let's pray."

Cassie thought about that while they said the closing prayer. She needed the Lord's direction on several things. What to do about the troublesome kids in her class? What should she do with her summer, her first free summer in years? Should she sell her parents' house? Should she take a few refresher classes at the University of Missouri at Kansas City?

"Do you want some coffee?" she asked Peter when the prayer ended. Peter was staring at someone across the room.

"In a minute. I've got to talk to someone." Peter shot away from Cassie like a baseball hit by a prime slugger.

He'd done it again! Left her standing alone. Miffed, she thought, just how much rudeness was she supposed to take?

She swung on her heel and stomped to the kitchen. They always needed help in the kitchen…and obviously, that was where she was best suited. Not with Peter!

Peter spotted Eric just about to slip out of the meeting. "Eric?"

Eric turned and hesitated. Peter took it as a good sign. At least Eric wasn't running away from him this time.

"Eric, can we talk?"

"Well, I don't know…."

"Please? We have so much to discuss."

"I'll stay a little while, I guess. But not long." Eric's stance was defensive as he gave in. "I have a wounded squirrel to see to."

"Yes…I understand." Though he didn't, Peter thought it best to pretend to understand Eric's needs. His brother was making excuses to withdraw if the conversation didn't please him, Peter thought.

"What did you want to say?" Eric asked.

"Oh, there's lots to cover. But we'll talk only of our father now, if you like."

Eric glanced away while making an uncaring shrug. For a scant moment it reminded Peter of his son. An unexpected pain shot though him, and traveled down his body as though he'd been struck by a bolt of lightning.

"Eric…." The name fell softly from his lips. "You're my only kin now. I had a son, did you know that? No…of course you didn't. He died seven—no, eight months ago. Of leukemia. I didn't… couldn't do anything to help him. Nothing."

At the news Eric glanced at him, a flicker of compassion in the depth of his eyes. Yet after he murmured an "I'm sorry," he remained silent.

Peter drew a deep breath. "I admit not knowing where you were didn't bother me much till then. I was too busy with the firm. The Tilford Real Estate firm while Dad was alive. Half of that belongs to you."

Eric stared at him as though he didn't understand.

"Haven't you ever heard of it?"

"No, I don't recall…only the vaguest memory. Did our…dad make a lot of money?"

Peter laughed humorlessly. "Yeah, he did. He wasn't much of a father, I'll grant you. But he was a success at business, and you're his son, same as me. Honestly, don't you know anything about Tilford and Associates?"

"Can't say I have."

Peter shook his head, a peculiar smile spreading. "Well, never mind that now. Dad always wanted you to have what was yours, even when he couldn't find you."

Eric stiffened. "I don't want any of it."

"But it's yours."

"Give it away." He made a deprecating gesture. "Give it to New Beginnings, if it's worth anything."

"If it's—?" Peter's jaw dropped, the knowledge of the more than half a million dollars lying about in banks drawing interest tickling his mind. Surely Eric didn't understand his inheritance.

"That's what I said."

"Don't you want to know how much it is?"

"No. Now I have to go see my patient."

Peter was losing him. Hurriedly, he

said, "Wait a minute. I'll walk out with you. You care for injured animals?"

"Yes, in my spare time."

"I know you work at a factory, but why didn't you go to veterinary school if you're interested in helping animals?"

They pushed through the church doors. Eric shrugged. "No money. I work with a guy that has a degree, though. He tells me I have a natural instinct for animals. I love the creatures. The work keeps me connected, you know?"

"Connected?"

"To my heavenly Father."

It was a subtle change from the discussion of their earthly father. Peter couldn't blame him.

Peter tried another tack. "I know little about animals." He glanced at his brother. "I'd like to learn, though."

The hint went unanswered. Instead, he said more urgently, "Listen, Eric, you could still go to school if you want that.

There's more than enough money for it, believe me."

Eric paused in the parking lot beside a beat-up Ford truck, staring into space. Then he turned slowly to gaze long and hard at Peter. Peter could barely make out his surprised expression.

"You wouldn't have to depend on me, honest. The money's there. It's yours. Dad wanted you to have it."

Eric dropped his gaze. "I've gotta go." Eric turned to climb into the truck.

"All right. But think about it, will you? Please?"

"Sure. See you around." Eric put the truck into gear and rolled out of the parking lot.

Peter stood looking at the retreating truck a moment, then shoved his hands in his pockets and strolled back into the church to grab some coffee. His brother was a stubborn Missouri mule. But he'd get to him yet.

He'd have to make it up to Cassie—

again. Yeah, more flowers, he guessed. But would that do it?

Nah…. He'd spend more time with her. That was what a woman usually wanted. But how would he find time?

Chapter Ten

Peter thought about his brother as he flew back to New York the next day. Eric didn't want anything of their father's, did he? Nothing. At least he didn't *think* he did. Well, Eric didn't know what he was giving up. Peter suspected he had no earthly knowledge of the size of the inheritance, but there was more than one way to skin a cat. More than one way to see that Eric received what was rightfully his. Let a little time pass and wear Eric down was one solution.

Other than that, Peter was frustrated at the slow progress he was making with

Eric. But then, he *was* making progress, he reminded himself. Eric hadn't totally shut him out. And he'd made a terrific suggestion concerning New Beginnings.

Giving the New Beginnings Ministry something appealed to him—but not just money. Although they could always use money, it would simply sink into a non-specific fund, he thought. But something solid… The idea found a fertile place in his mind. Something that Eric could get into…

He'd never visited the Lake of the Ozarks, but he understood it to be a major recreational area for the Midwest. What if he found some land there to give New Beginnings? Or a house of some kind. It could use a place to go for retreats and such. Yes, land for the New Beginnings crowd would do the trick.

He picked up his phone. "This is Peter…give me Bill West."

A few moments later, he was satisfied he'd put the plan into motion. By the time he reached his desk in New York, information of every suitable piece of land for sale on the lake would be there. He'd surely find something.

Later that day, Cassie slowly chewed her hard-boiled egg, listening with half an ear to the other teachers' chatter, while thinking of Peter. Even though he'd promised, explanations hadn't materialized.

Where did he spend his time when he wasn't with her? He'd said he was working. But she hadn't seen his motorcycle for weeks, and he didn't eat regularly. Their meals together proved that. He was always hungry, twice admitting he hadn't eaten earlier in the day.

Maybe he didn't have the money to eat three meals a day.

Perhaps that overheard conversation was a blessing. What was it about exactly? If the deal didn't materialize the next morning, he'd walk? What did that mean? What if his job depended on that deal—whatever it was? Did that mean he didn't draw a regular paycheck?

"Why are you frowning?" asked Donna, sitting in the chair next to her. "What's up?"

"Oh, was I? It's nothing. I'm just not very hungry."

"Boy, I am," chimed in Jacqueline, the permanent substitute. "Those kids wear me out. I don't think I'm cut out to be a teacher of young ones."

"I love the little ones," Liz spoke up. "As long as I can send them home in the middle of the afternoon."

"Perhaps you should apply at the high school…." Jacqueline's voice trailed away.

"This is where I came in," Cassie whispered to Donna.

"Seems that way," Donna whispered back.

Cassie let the thread of conversation go

on without her. She gathered up the remains of her lunch, leaving the potato chips unopened, and wandered out of the lunch room. She strolled out the side door and rested against the doorjamb, watching the students play. The bell would ring in a few minutes, and she should be going through the latest history papers.

But all she could think about was Peter.

Had he lost his job? All the evidence seemed to point that way. He hadn't mentioned buying a place for more than a month. He was skipping meals. He'd spent money on three dozen roses to dazzle her into forgiving him for being rude, when he didn't have enough to make it from week to week. He'd insisted on paying the dinner bill the other night, and then when they arrived at New Beginnings, he'd been rude again.

What was that about, anyway?

More puzzling, and more hurtful, he'd found a ride home with Pastor Mike, forgetting he'd left his phone behind at her house. His promised explanation of what was bothering him had never come. Perhaps he didn't really trust her. What was he hiding? Did he drink to excess? Or gamble his paycheck away?

She'd stared at that phone this morning, silently wishing it into the deepest part of the lake. It had rung a couple of times. She'd ignored it at first—after all, it wasn't her phone. Then just as she walked out the door for the morning, she snatched it up when it rang.

"Hello?"

"May I speak to Peter, please?" A female voice had sounded young.

"Um, he isn't here. May I take a message?"

"Is this Cassie?"

"Yes."

"Well, I'm glad to catch you. Please

tell Peter that the closing on the condo will take place in a month. I'll call with the exact day and time. But it's all set."

"Oh, um, thank you. Thank you for calling."

"You bet."

She hadn't thought about it until now. Peter had bought a condo? Was that what he was going to confide in her? But he could've said that in the few moments they had been driving together to New Beginnings. What was the problem?

Perhaps he thought it would be too much information if he told her he was out of work. Then another thought struck her. Did he think… *was* he taking advantage of her? Of her obvious lack of sophistication?

An uneasy disquiet shot through her, and she straightened from the doorway and practically ran down the hall to her classroom.

She really liked Peter. A lot. She tried

to put her hurt feelings aside, but she thought it would take more than a few days or a casual apology to cover it. Yet what could she base her feelings on? The fact that he'd chosen her to hang out with those few times when he was in town? Or that he now chose someone else to confide in? Pastor Mike was, after all, a better choice, she admitted, and a trained counselor. Perhaps Peter needed a professional. After all, she didn't own Peter Scott, did she?

Oh, Lord, I don't know what Peter's problems are, but they seem to be many. Please help him. Let him hear Your directions for his life. And let me not take it too personally....

The bell rang and the children streamed into the room. Thankfully, she was forced to put her thoughts aside, and she took a deep breath to concentrate on the rest of the day. "Get out your math books, children. Let's do a little preparing for the final tests that will be coming up in a couple of weeks. You've done wonderfully well up to now, but there's one or two areas I'd like us to review."

With that, her afternoon was set. Whether Peter Scott was to be a continuing part of her life or not was up to the Lord.

But oh, she hoped Peter wouldn't fade away!

Late in the day on Thursday, Pam, Maggie and she had reservations at Ethan's Place, Lisa and Ethan's restaurant. They met at the church, then climbed into Maggie's car and drove together to the site. When they entered, Lisa met them at the door.

"Hello, ladies, how are you? It's so nice to see some of the New Beginnings crowd."

"Nice to see you, Lisa," Pam answered, gazing about. "And so successful!"

"Thanks, girls. That's what we want to hear," Lisa said with a smile.

"This is a lovely place," Maggie said. The restaurant was decorated in an old-world style with tablecloths, cloth napkins and soft music in the background. Diners occupied a few tables, but the place was only half full. "Where's Ethan?"

"He's in the kitchen, but I'll get him to come out to say hello in a bit. I'm glad you're early, before the rush. This way you can have a choice of tables."

"We came early on purpose, so that we can get to New Beginnings on time. How about that one?" said Cassie. She nodded toward a table in the rear corner. "Then we can talk all we want to and not disturb anyone."

"Right you are," Lisa said with a smile, and led them back.

"Oh, this is nice," murmured Cassie, thinking Peter would like it.

Other customers came in, and Lisa left to greet them. The three women opened their menus.

"When are we going shopping again?" Maggie asked. "I need to get something for summer. I'm going to Europe for two weeks if I have to spend all my savings."

"Europe?" Pam groaned. "I'd love a trip to Europe. But I don't think I can go shopping anytime soon."

"Well, I need new shoes," remarked Maggie. "Can't you manage just half a day?"

"Hmm...well, maybe."

"I'd love to go. School is out next week, then I'm free for the summer," Cassie said.

"Wish I was, but all I have are two weeks of vacation," said Maggie, scrunching up her mouth. "You don't have anyone at home, do you, Cassie? You live alone?"

Cassie looked up from her menu. "Yes, since my father passed away."

"That's what I thought. Are you going somewhere on vacation?"

"I don't think so. I thought of going on

one of those singles cruises, perhaps down to Panama City or such."

"Sounds great," Pam remarked with a sigh. "I'd go in a minute if I could get away. Why don't you?"

"I wouldn't know anyone to go with. Traveling on my own doesn't sound like much fun."

Ethan came out of the kitchen and strolled to their table, bringing three dishes with him. "Hiya, ladies. Have you ordered yet?"

"No, we've been too busy talking."

"Well, before you do, you must try these dishes I'm about to add to the menu. Then you can tell me how you like them. I know it's Thursday. How's New Beginnings coming along?"

"It's fine, but we miss you and Lisa," said Maggie. "It's not the same without you and your guitar."

"Yeah, we miss it, too. The best we can do is attend services on Sunday mornings. Perhaps we can visit some

Thursday soon, after we're sure the restaurant can do without us for a night.
But I'm going to play a little later. Can
you stay for a few moments of that?"

"Well, we'll see, but it'll be close
timing," Pam replied.

"Ethan?"

"Someone calls. Be sure to tell me if
you like these dishes. And be sure to tell
everyone we said hello, okay?"

With that he hurried off.

The three women gazed at the
generous dishes he'd laid on their table.
Lasagna in a rich-looking sauce, shrimp
Alfredo and something that resembled a
glorified burger patty.

"If we eat all that, we won't want to
order," Cassie murmured in wonder.

"We can always take what's left over
home," commented Maggie with a
giggle, staring at the food. "Or to New
Beginnings. Those folks eat anything
and everything."

"True," muttered Pam, grinning. "That's

a great idea, and it'll be great advertising for them. Let's order. The food won't go to waste."

Later, entering the New Beginnings room in plenty of time for the meeting, they began to dish out their food in tiny portions so that everyone could have a bite. Cassie was reaching for the paper plates for dessert when she heard Peter's voice. Then Pastor Mike, murmuring an answer.

Two Thursday nights in a row? Peter was really making an effort to attend their meetings.

But he hadn't let her know he was coming….

She peeked out from the kitchen door. Pastor Mike headed toward the front, while Peter glanced about. When he spotted her, he came into the kitchen. Hurriedly, she turned back to cutting up the lasagna.

"Cassie, I tried to call. Where have you been?" Peter sounded a bit irritated.

Surprised, Cassie clipped out, "Out."

His mouth tightened. "All right, I deserved that. Why don't you have a cell phone like everyone else?"

"I—" She raised her chin. "I can't afford one."

"Why not?"

Looking about, only Pam was within hearing distance. It wouldn't matter, anyway. She had nothing to hide.

"I'm still paying for Dad's funeral, for one thing, and his last hospital bill, my car payment, and I'm saving for the taxes I'll owe. When I get those first two paid off, then maybe I'll think about it."

"Excuse me." Pam lowered her head and scooted out of the kitchen.

Peter stared at Cassie, looking flustered. "Um…I'm sorry, Cassie." Then in a gentle tone, "Guess I shouldn't presume you'll always be waiting."

"No, you shouldn't."

"Okay. Gotcha. Now can we get back to being friends?"

Friends? Was that all they had, friend-ship? "Yeah, sure."

He studied her a moment, frustrated. "I've got to see Eric Landers…if he's here tonight. He's my brother, Cassie. My half brother that I hadn't seen in forty years—until coming to New Beginnings. That's why I've been so distracted lately…."

Cassie's anger melted as what he was telling her sunk in. Peter and Eric? Brothers? That was the secret he'd been hiding? That was the real reason for him behaving so irrationally?

She stopped laying out cups. "The meeting is starting, Peter." She looked at him, at his sky-blue eyes, and said in a quiet tone, "Your explanations can come later. And I *do* want to hear them."

She always gave her mischievous students three tries to straighten up if they could before sending them to the principal's office. Peter was on his third grace period. She hid her sigh as Pastor

Mike began the night's program with prayer, then silently was amused when she realized she'd equated Peter with a student. Ah, well….

"Abide in me…" Pastor Mike began his talk. "Jesus says 'Live in me…'"

At the close, Pastor Mike said, "Now before we go, I have something else to discuss. I need your full attention. We have been given—that is, New Beginnings has been given—a place down on the Lake of the Ozarks."

A collective gasp, along with "You're kidding" and "Really?" erupted from the crowd.

"Sure 'nuff," Pastor Mike answered. "It's a small lodge of some sort along with about ten acres of land. Now if I understand correctly, the deal's not quite complete yet, but we need a committee to go down to see it. To tell us if the place will do. It's kind of old and in need of repair, and with the newer laws concerning the dock floats and things, that'll cost a bundle to replace, but we need to see what's being offered. Do we have volunteers?"

Seven hands shot up.

"That's great." Pastor Mike said, glancing around at who could go. "Can you go on Saturday?"

Two hands dropped.

"Okay, that narrows it down. Four men—Chris, Charlie, Jason and Eric—and one woman, Lori. Hmm… Can we have another female volunteer?"

Pam nudged Cassie. "You should go."

"Me?" Her mouth dropped. "The idea hadn't occurred to me."

"You don't have anyone at home to demand your attention. Why not? And someone needs to keep Lori, um, balanced, I'm thinking."

"You're right." Cassie's arm shot up.

Giggling, Cassie put her other hand over her mouth. Keeping a lid on Lori was an awesome task, but she thought she could do it, if it came to that. She was learning the art of a cordial put-down. Otherwise, the idea of going did appeal to Cassie. This would be the change of pace she was looking for.

"Okay, Cassie," Pastor Mike said. "You and Lori, Chris, Eric, Jason and Charlie." Pastor Mike made notes, then looked up again. "Chris, since you work in home repair, that's good. You can tell us what repairs we need to consider. Jason, you can tell us if the plumbing system is up to par. See me at the close of the meeting, and we'll arrange things."

Cassie turned around in her chair and stared at Peter. She tipped her head and widened her eyes. Why didn't he volunteer? If his business was iffy…or if he'd lost his job…

It would be a perfect opportunity to spend time with Eric! Wasn't that what he wanted? Was he too proud to say anything? His eyes looked bluer than ever as he returned her stare without expression, shrugging.

He didn't want to go down, that was it. Hiding her disappointment, Cassie stared forward while the closing prayer was said.

Eric sat in the front of the meeting, on the side. He rose slowly, glancing warily toward Peter.

Wait! Peter thought. *Don't rush him again. Let him come to you....* Now that Eric knew who he was, Peter was willing to wait, though patience wasn't one of his virtues. He held Eric's gaze as the other man strolled toward him—not too reluctantly, Peter noticed.

Peter shoved his hands in his pockets, so very glad his brother was at least willing to talk. "How's it going?"

"Fine." Eric didn't rush out, or past him. He actually paused to talk to him—though he looked at everything and everyone beside Peter. His spirits lifted. Others milled around them waiting for coffee and dessert.

"Any patients at home?"

"Not at the moment."

"Interesting vocation, taking care of wild animals. Never was into animals, myself. Had a dog once, long ago. A toy collie—do you recall her? Scrappy?"

Eric frowned slightly. "Only vaguely. Was she afraid of thunderstorms?"

"Yes, she sure was." His voice became nostalgic. "She used to hide under my bed when it thundered." Then he added, "Dad gave her to the cook after I went to school."

"Coffee?" asked Cassie, carrying a tray.

"Sure." Peter took a cup at the same time as Eric. "Thanks. And some of that pie, whatever kind it is."

"There are samples of Ethan's cooking on the table," Cassie offered. "But you'd better hurry. They're going fast."

"Sounds good." He craned his neck to view the offerings. He was hungry, but he didn't want to leave Eric. "I'll get some later. Does that mean I can't have any pie?"

"Sure. But if you tell me you didn't eat dinner again, I'm going to wring your neck. You skip far too many meals for your good health."

"Um, then I won't tell you that!" His blue eyes twinkled as Lori joined them. Lori opened her mouth to speak, but Cassie didn't give her a chance.

"You mean you *did* skip dinner? What am I going to do with you? Why do you do that, Peter? Go without eating? You know, you really should eat something substantial, not just pie and coffee."

Maggie swung their way with a tray of lemon meringue and apple pie slices and the men each took a serving.

"If I tell you I skipped supper, as well, will you scold me, too?" asked Eric, entering into the fun. He took a large bite of apple pie.

Cassie looked from one to the other. The two of them were teasing, but she wasn't. "Oh, you two! Being a bachelor doesn't excuse you from skipping meals, you know. You act like two foolish teens! You should take better care of yourselves! It seems to me you could manage even frozen pizza or a sandwich, or something."

Peter threw back his head and laughed. Eric chuckled. They thought this a joke? At her expense?

She just had to push it, she couldn't help herself. "Honestly, you need a—a cook or someone...."

"I need someone to look after me," remarked Peter, still smiling.

"You certainly do!"

"Will you take on the task?"

Cassie blushed furiously. "What do you mean?"

"Oh, I don't know. Be my personal assistant or something. You could see that Eric and I eat regularly. Set a bedtime. Get enough sleep." His smile spread wider as he glanced at Eric. Eric returned the glance. She noticed the similarity of their eyes.

Was Peter telling her that he was announcing that Eric and he were brothers? It seemed so. Eric's eyes lit.

"Oh, sure." She rolled her eyes while Eric gently laughed again. Peter grinned, his eyes merry.

Lori sighed in disgust at not joining the conversation, and walked away. Pam stopped in her tracks, and watched them with her mouth ajar. Maggie giggled uproariously. Heads turned their way.

"Now that's a job I'd just love to have." Cassie didn't use sarcasm often, but her feelings now ran away with her. "Looking after the two of you would be worse than looking after my fifth-graders. You'd be in trouble all the time. You guys eat while I go talk to Pastor Mike."

Cassie walked away. Peter was so—so provoking! And now his brother was getting in on the act?

Chapter Eleven

At two minutes past eight o'clock on Saturday morning, Cassie pulled up to the church parking lot to see a small group of people waiting beside the church van.

"Am I the last one here?" she asked as she shut her car door. She wore a new pair of knee-length dark-red shorts and a striped top, and she hoped she looked smart.

"Yeah. We've been waiting for all of five minutes," teased Chris, making a show of glancing at his watch. Cassie thought Chris was cute, in a young sort of way. His light-blond hair added to his youthful look.

"I've been here fifteen minutes already," Lori stated with a superior air, a dark eyebrow raised. She wasn't teasing at all. "We're supposed to leave promptly at eight."

Then Pastor Mike stepped aside, and Cassie saw Peter standing next to Eric.

"Peter! Why, I thought—that is, you weren't supposed to be here today. Don't you have somewhere else to be?"

"Not today. Not this weekend. I'm going with you all."

"That's nice," she mumbled out. Then she realized he'd be spending all his time with Eric.

Well, of course he would want to get to know his brother better. Anyone would after the long separation the two had experienced. She pushed her confused emotions into the back of her mind.

But a little part of her wondered if she

was now to be ignored. Was Peter's interest in her over?

She steadied her gaze on Pastor Mike.

"Okay, everyone's here," Pastor Mike remarked. "We can take the church's van. There's just enough seats for all of us."

She let the others climb into the van first, noticing Lori squeezing herself next to Peter and Eric in the last seat. She found herself between Chris and beefy Charlie in the second seat. She scooted over an inch, looking for her seat belt.

"Do you know how old this place is?" asked Jason, as he adjusted his seat belt. Jason, rather new to the group, occupied the front seat with Pastor Mike. He ran a hand through his cropped hair.

"I understand it was built around 1950 for a family named Harris." Pastor Mike turned on the motor and drove out of the parking lot. "They sold it to the Holt clan, who ran it as a hunting and fishing lodge for a few years. I tried to find out if anyone from our church had ever been there, but no luck. Then the place sat idle for awhile, and now it's come to us."

Behind her, Lori tried to engage Eric and Peter in conversation. She pointed out the window. "The gardens are wonderful this year. Look at those roses on the terrace."

"We've had enough rain," Eric answered. "All the gardens are good."

"How did that happen?" Jason asked of Pastor Mike.

"Ah, the gift came out of the blue. It's specifically for the New Beginnings ministry, but I imagine any one of the church groups may use it. It's wonderful. But it needs a little work, I understand. We'll see how much when we get there."

Cassie listened to both conversations in silence.

"But you don't know who gave it?" Jason questioned.

"The donor wishes to remain anonymous," Pastor Mike replied. "It's mighty generous though."

"I'll say. No matter what shape the place is in, we can use it," Chris added. "Imagine! A place on the lake."

"Did you see in the paper…?" Lori's tone was even, talking about something else entirely.

The male voices blended, and Cassie ceased to listen. It no longer mattered that Lori had Peter's attention. It wasn't her, and she refused to recognize the hurt it caused her. Cassie decided she'd join her seatmate's conversation.

"If it only needs paint, I can manage that. I have two months of real freedom this summer, and I can certainly put in some time if Chris shows me how. What I want to know is if the plumbing is okay. I don't relish putting up with poor plumbing."

"Don't know, Cassie. But we have Jason here," Pastor Mike said. "That's why I brought him. And Chris, you, too."

"Yeah, if the plumbing needs work, I can take care of it," said Jason. "If it was built in the fifties, I expect it'll need lots of it. Can we afford the remodeling?"

"Well, the gift includes some money for updating. Don't know how far it'll go," the pastor remarked.

"Sure, Cassie, I'll show you," Chris mumbled in Cassie's ear, his expression flirtatious and interested.

Her emotions rose and Cassie smiled at Chris. Behind her, she heard a gruff "hrumph."

Was that Peter? She didn't dare turn around to look at him.

Only an old sign on a post with ten other signs told them they had arrived. The van took the narrower blacktop road about a quarter of a mile, with offshoots of other lake addresses. The long road became narrower and turned to dirt and gravel. Finally, their destination was the only one the road serviced. They drove up and over a large hill, and there it stood next to the blue of lake water. A two-storied structure, much bigger than any of them had expected, sat majestically against the hill.

Pastor Mike brought the van to a stop. "Oh, my!" They all stared.

"That's it?" Jason gasped.

"Only a lodge?" Chris added, his mouth half open. "It's a mansion!"

Lori scooted forward to get a better view. "Let's get out. I can't see."

"We'll be there in a jiff," said Pastor Mike, starting to release the brake.

"But I want to get the full view now," Lori complained.

For once, Cassie agreed with Lori. "Yes, let's."

Charlie eagerly swung his door wide, and they all scrambled to get out of the car. "Yes, I think we'd better get out here, to see what we've really got," said Charlie, full of awe. "This is more than we thought."

They all stood at the top of the hill, staring.

"I'm going to walk down," said Chris.

Cassie glanced at Peter and Eric. Eric gazed at the woods edging the property, his expression far away. Peter watched him, a slight smile on his face. He then looked around him, watching the faces of the committee.

"I'll go with you," Cassie suddenly decided as Chris started off down the hill. The brush was thick, but Cassie resolutely followed. Hearing the voices fading, she glanced over her shoulder. A dozen feet behind, Eric was walking, too. And Peter.

She bit her lip. Peter wasn't here to look after her. No, they were all here to work.

Well, she could look after herself! And she was doing that, wasn't she? Learning new things, new ways of being social. She had no one to tie her down anymore.

The van passed them, but the walkers caught up in the circle drive. The carved front door stood open.

Cassie followed Chris inside. Peter and Eric crowded behind them. Lori, Jason and the pastor stood in the wide slate-floor front hall, gazing about them. The open hall looked over the empty blue-carpeted living room. The stairs wound up one side, overlooking the huge two-storied room, which boasted twin bricked fireplaces, one on either end. The dining room was two steps down at the back on one side. Cassie supposed the kitchen was beyond.

She wondered what could be seen from the wide picture windows on the back wall, and strolled there to see.

Peter followed with Eric. They stared out at the lake, a breathless expanse of blue water. Cabins and houses sat on the banks opposite, and a motorboat buzzed out to the main channel.

"Pretty," said Peter, his hands in his pockets.

"Yeah...it's lovely," Cassie replied.

"Six bedrooms, I'm told," murmured

Pastor Mike to no one in particular. "Two to a bedroom will give us only room for twelve at a time. But this room will be ideal for gatherings. We can get, oh, possibly thirty people in here with comfort."

"If we can get some furniture," said Chris, looking about at the stripped walls. Nothing but a couple of ugly brown chairs occupied the room. "And it does need some paint."

"I've got an old couch we can bring down," offered Charlie.

"I can just imagine what your old couch would look like," said Lori. "We need furniture, all right, but I'm thinking we need fresh, comfortable stuff."

"I don't think our budget will support that. Well, maybe a few pieces," said Pastor Mike. It wasn't like him to sound so uncertain, and Cassie turned from the window to glance at him. His gaze, looking guilty or secretive, suddenly went everywhere over the room as he murmured, "Let's look at the rest of the house."

What was up with him? Cassie wondered.

"The wood on these windows is rotting. We'll need to replace it." Chris stood next to Cassie, his fingers rubbing a windowsill. Paint and rotted wood came up from the corner. "Wonder where else there's been rot. Come on, Cassie. We'll be window inspectors."

"All right. We'll count as we go."

"The kitchen is through here," shouted Lori, out of sight through the dining room. A large blond oak table and eight chairs remained there, and she remarked, "At least we have somewhere to sit while we eat."

"Might as well start there," Chris said. He grinned at Cassie, and grabbed her hand. "C'mon, Cassie. Let's see."

Cassie glanced at Peter over her shoulder as they reached the two steps down. Peter stared at her with a funny, speculative look on his face. Odd, not funny, she thought. What was on his mind? she wondered.

She pulled her hand free from Chris as they swung through the dining room and into the kitchen. He paid little attention. She didn't have time to analyze it now, but she hadn't felt anything but friendship at Chris's touch. Not like Peter's.

A sudden memory of Peter's kiss came to mind. A rush of emotion made her want to smile, and she turned away to hide her blushing cheeks.

The kitchen was a large, old-fashioned room, but it had newer appliances. Two stoves and a huge refrigerator looked to be only a couple of years old. A microwave oven sat in the corner, but there was no dishwasher.

"Looks like we'll have to do dishes by hand," said Cassie. "But that's not a problem, really."

"Well, I'll leave that to you." Lori ran her hand over the old counter. Jason pulled open the oven doors, and Lori peered into them. "But it looks like it all could use a good cleaning."

"We can solve that easily. Why is it so dark in here?" Cassie asked. Only a couple of windows over the sink let in light. She stared at the ceiling, which showed a water stain in the corner.

"Um, I guess because no one has turned on the power," said Peter, right behind her. Eric had gone out the back door; Pastor Mike was opening the empty cupboards, as Charlie looked under the sink.

"Oh. Of course. Well, where is it?"

"I expect in the basement. But we'll have to call the power company if this place has been closed up a while. Hmm, where is the basement?" Peter turned in a half circle and spotted a door.

"I'll go and see," said Jason, pulling out a flashlight. "Want to come, Charlie?"

"Sure," Charlie replied. "Might as well."

"I'll come, too," said Peter. "Cassie?"

"Sure. I want to see it all."

They inspected the huge basement, which had a Ping-Pong table and a couple of odd chairs in the corner. A row of shelving lined one wall. Jason first went to the power box, and threw some switches. From above, they heard a shout.

"The power is on."

"That's good," Jason remarked. "Somebody's been looking after the place."

The basement lights went on, and Carrie turned to see Peter inspecting the furnace. "Wish I knew what I was looking for, but I'd say this furnace is pretty old. Wouldn't need it in the summer, of course, but the place would get mighty cold in the winter without heat."

"There's the two fireplaces," Cassie remarked.

"Yes, but that wouldn't be enough to heat the entire house," Jason said.

"Well, we have all summer to work on it," said Charlie.

Upstairs again, Cassie and Lori decided to inspect the bedrooms. After they were done, they met Pastor Mike coming out of the bedroom Cassie had seen earlier. "Well, what do you think?" he inquired.

"I think it's a wonderful place," Cassie enthused, running her hand along an old-fashioned hall table.

"It has a boathouse down at the water," Eric called, coming through the back door. "But no boats."

They started down the stairs. Cassie felt a hand at her elbow, and turned to find Peter there. A warm glance met hers.

"So you like this place."

"I sure do. I think we can—"

An "oomph" came from behind, and she felt something hit her in the back. Off guard, she started to fall. Peter grabbed her other arm, saving her from tumbling down the stairs.

"What—?" Cassie swiftly turned to hear a moan. Lori lay on the stairs, her hands splayed behind her.

Pastor Mike knelt beside her. "Oh! Oh, my. Are you all right?"

"I guess so," said Lori, a little dazed. She put her hand to her head. "I'm not usually so clumsy. My foot caught on the edge of the carpet, and I lost my balance."

"The stair carpet is ragged here," Peter offered. "We need to replace it."

"You're very lucky, Lori. You could have fallen all the way down," uttered Cassie.

"Yes, I— You broke the fall, Cassie. Thanks."

"I guess…I mean, I almost fell, too. But Peter caught me. I think we should thank Peter!"

She glanced at Peter as she spoke. His blue eyes shone with commiseration, sparked with humor.

"Well, are you both all right?" the pastor asked, glancing at both women.

"I twisted my ankle a little, I think," muttered Lori, sinking to sit on the stairs. Her mouth tightened with pain. "It sure hurts. And I hit my hand as I fell, trying to break my fall. I can't seem to use it."

"Here, let's see. Hmm…" Pastor Mike examined the ankle, then her wrist. "We'll have to see about an X-ray."

"I've worked as a paramedic the past five years. Let me see," said Chris, coming forward from the kitchen. He went to his heels and slipped off Lori's sandal. Gingerly, he felt the ankle while Lori hissed. "Yeah, I think we need to find an emergency room."

Peter had his cell phone out before Chris had finished speaking. He listened, muttered something into the phone, then snapped it closed. "Okay, it's not too far. Let's go."

Peter called to rest of the group, who were out on the sundeck.

Jason and Chris carried Lori out to

the car while Pastor Mike closed the house. They made their trip to a twenty-four-hour medical clinic on the main highway and waited their turn. A woman and small boy waited in the corner, and an old man took up a chair next to the door.

The old man stared at Peter a long time. Recognition shone from his eyes. "Hey, aren't you Peter Tilford?" he finally asked. "What in the world are you doing in a little place like this?"

The old man continued, "Say, I saw your old man once. In New York. I was working there for a few months, and I was doing business with the law firm Bledsoe and Conners. You was just a kid then, but I never forget a face. You are Peter Tilford, aren't you?"

"Yes, I'm Peter Tilford. I'm here with some friends, looking at property."

The doctor came out of his office and called for Oscar Paddington, and the old man said, "That's me, folks. Say, if you're interested in property down here, let me know. I might be interested in some next to you, if you know what I mean?"

"I'd appreciate if you'd keep quiet about seeing me down here, Oscar. Don't want to start any, um, rumors or anything, you know."

"You can count on me, Mr. Tilford." The old man disappeared down the doctor's hall.

"Peter?" asked Lori. "What was he talking about?"

Peter sighed. "I guess the secret is out of the bag now."

"What secret?" asked Cassie.

"About who I am. And what I'm involved in. My company is Tilford Enterprises, a real estate company. We deal in high-priced companies and real estate. We're also a leading land developer of upscale condos and houses. I do business mainly on the East Coast,

Florida and in Europe. Can we drop the subject now?"

"Yes, I've heard of you!" Lori said in awe. You're that Peter Tilford?"

"Yes. But I'd appreciate if you'd forget it. At New Beginnings, I'm just one of you."

"It's after two," Pastor Mike said, looking at his watch. "I'm starved, and I imagine everyone else is, too. There's a sandwich shop down the hill. I'll go get us some."

"Good idea. I'll go, too," offered Charlie.

Lori muttered, "Always thinking of your stomachs, huh?"

"It'll make the time go faster for them," Cassie whispered to Lori, as Peter gazed at her from across the room. "Men get cranky when they haven't eaten. The doctor will work through his patient load soon. He'll have you all fixed up in no time."

"Yeah, I guess." Lori raised her voice.

"Bring me back a turkey on whole wheat if you can get it."

"I'll wait outside, if you don't mind," Peter said.

"I'll wait with Lori," Cassie said. The three men left, then after a moment, so did Peter and Eric. Cassie offered, "Let me get you some water."

"Thanks."

Cassie's tone was sympathetic. Once or twice she'd had to keep a child's spirits up while they waited for medical attention. She held her smile. Lori was a far cry from a child, but still, everyone needed a little sympathy when they were hurting.

Soon, Lori was called before the men returned. Cassie helped her up from her chair and Lori hopped into the examining room. Just before she entered, Lori turned to Cassie. "Come in with me. Please?"

"Sure," Cassie said, feeling glad she could help.

An hour later, they carefully climbed

back into the van, Lori in the middle seat with Jason and Chris.

"Glad it's only a sprain, Lori," muttered Chris. "But you'll have to stay off it for a day or two."

Pastor Mike spoke. "Well, what do you guys want to do? Start for home immediately? Or there's a little roadside park a couple of miles distant. We can stop and eat our sandwiches there."

"That sounds good to me," Chris said. "If Lori is up to it."

"Yeah. I'm starved. Let's do that," Charlie agreed.

Cassie looked at Lori. "Are you up to that?"

"Sure. As long as I stay off my feet." She glanced longingly at Peter. "But I don't know what I'll do when I get home. Maybe you could…"

"I've called your sister," said Pastor Mike. "She's going to meet us at the church at about five-thirty or six."

"Oh, um, thank you, but…"

"That's perfect, because Cassie and I have dinner plans," said Peter.

They did? Cassie stared at him. Could Peter be…jealous?

Chapter Twelve

"The dock will take some work," Lori said, munching on her sandwich.

She seemed to have forgotten the new information they'd learned about Peter. The pain pills the clinic had given her were working. Lori was positively happy. "It looks as if there's a good place for sunbathing and swimming."

"But the furnace is old and needs replacing," added Jason, reaching for the chips. "We need to get that taken care of before winter. I could install it, if we had the money for that."

"Mmm...I'll see." Pastor Mike shook

his head. "Don't know if our donor is ready for all that."

"Pastor Mike, can't we use the place and work on it a little at a time?" asked Charlie, swinging his leg over the wooden seat. "We don't need air-conditioning or anything for now."

The pastor brightened. "I don't see why not. We could organize a few weekend work parties. We can hold services there on Sunday mornings out in the field, if Reverend Hostetter okays it. I don't think the Lord cares where, as long as we worship Him. It will give us wonderful opportunity for fellowship and study."

"Yes, let's propose that to the church," Cassie said, sitting next to Peter and Eric. "Surely the church leaders wouldn't object. I'm sure several of the New Beginnings crowd are eager to come on weekends. School's out for summer, and it's a great time for me to be down there through the week, but I don't know if anyone else could spend real time here."

"I've got a couple of weeks of vacation coming," offered Chris. "I wasn't planning on going anywhere. I'd be real happy to spend it down here, and if Jason wants to install a new furnace, I'll help."

"Me, too," Eric chimed in. "What's the chance of my coming down a couple of weekends now, and a full week in July?"

Peter's attention was glued on Eric, while Jason and Charlie talked of the suggestion. "July, huh? That would work for me, too…if you have no objections?"

"I guess not," Eric replied. "Um…do you really want to come then?"

"I sure do," Peter replied, his eyes sparkling.

"How about you, Cassie?" Pastor Mike asked.

"Sure, July is fine with me." Cassie nodded, wondering what it would be like to spend several days in a row with Peter. "As I say, I have the whole summer free."

"The whole summer, eh?" Peter murmured for her ears alone. "That's what I like to hear."

"Why is that?" Cassie said. "What are you doing this summer? You haven't mentioned work…. Do you have a project or something? Can you manage to give the Ozarks a whole week of your time?"

"A project? I guess you could say." Peter lowered his eyes and shot Cassie a subtle gaze. "I guess I can free up my schedule for a week if you and Eric are going then."

"Fine. How about the first week in July? That'll be over the holiday weekend, you know," said Cassie.

"I'm looking forward to it." Peter made the statement as if it were a done deal. As if he meant it.

The ride home was quiet. Charlie and Chris sat in the middle row with Lori, so she could prop her ankle over their knees. Cassie sat in the other row, on the window seat with Peter, and Eric on Peter's other side. Peter slid his arm along the back of the seat, almost cupping Cassie's shoulders, and she drifted off.

Cassie woke up about thirty minutes later, her head on Peter's shoulder. She must have fallen asleep. She stirred and discovered her hand was in Peter's. It felt warm and comforting.

"Feel better?" he asked, smiling slightly. Cassie's heart skipped a beat. How could the man be so charming one moment, and totally irritating the next?

"Yes, I guess I do." She sat up, pulling down her knit top, which had crept up. "Sorry I went to sleep. I was up late last night cleaning out my father's closet."

"A sad chore." Peter's tone sounded sincere. "I lost my only son about eight months ago. I… haven't finished grieving. When did your dad pass away?"

"About six months ago." Peter had a

son? This was the first he'd mentioned it. No wonder she caught a sad glance from him once in a while. Perhaps it was time to change the subject? "Say, Pastor Mike, do you know of anyone who could use a wheelchair?"

"Yeah, I have a number of organizations you can call," Pastor Mike answered from the driver's seat. "They're always glad to accept donations."

"Good," she murmured. She could donate old clothes, too. Lots of old clothes, hers as well as her father's. She glanced forward to see how Lori was making out. She seemed to be slumped against Chris.

"Almost home," Peter remarked, low. "Want to grab some dinner later?"

"Um, yeah, but we ate lunch so late."

"Later's not a problem for me. I'll stop by around seven or so. Okay?"

"Sure, seven it is." Cassie had a better idea. She'd *make* dinner. Then they could have a nice long talk and maybe

Peter would be willing to share more about his life with her.

Soon they were pulling up in the church parking lot. "I hope your ankle feels better by morning, Lori. Do you have someone to call if you need anything?"

"Yes, my sister will take care of me. Don't worry about me. And, Cassie... thanks for all your help back at the clinic. I really appreciate it."

Lori's tone was kinder than usual. Cassie smiled. "That's okay. Glad to do it."

A few hours later, Cassie checked the dining room table with satisfaction. The good china, silver flatware and cloth napkins made the table look grand. The years since her mother had last set the table seemed to float away.

When the doorbell sounded, she hurried to let Peter in. He strolled inside, offering her a small bouquet of mixed spring flowers as he eyed the table. "We're eating here?

"I thought I would return the favor of dinner," Cassie said as she untied her apron, and offered Peter to be seated in her father's place. It didn't seem odd at all, she thought, to see Peter there, as she brought the food to the table. They ate in peaceful silence.

After dinner, Peter settled on the couch, and she cleared the table with ease. She stacked the dishes neatly beside the sink to tackle later. Right now she wanted to visit with Peter. Just talk. Nothing more.

Peter was relaxed. He'd kicked off his shoes and turned on the TV, watching a news program with half-closed eyelids.

She set a cup of coffee in front of him. "Tired?"

"Yeah. It's been a hard week for me."

"I'm sure, what with discovering your brother and all. Have you and he been able to talk?"

"No. He doesn't want to talk, it seems.

Every time we start connecting, either he pulls away or we're interrupted. We need somewhere quiet where we can talk where no one can interrupt us."

"What is so urgent?" Cassie asked.

"Well…sit down, will you, Cassie?" he asked plaintively.

Cassie sat on the end of her sofa, then turned to look at him. She was silent, waiting.

"Cassie…my dad was wealthy, and when he died, he divided his small fortune equally between his two sons. I put Eric's money in a safe bank account and it built to a sizeable sum. He'll have complete control over it now. I took my half and made it grow for me. I built Tilford Enterprises with it. I'm very, very wealthy. I have more money than Donald Trump."

Cassie just stared at him in his confession. Then, "You're joking!"

"Not a whit!"

"You're rich?" She jerked up and started pacing the floor. "How could you be? You barely had enough money to pay for dinner a couple of times. Why, I…I wanted to cook tonight to save you from embarrassment! And now you tell me you have money?" She whirled on her heel to stare at him. "How could you lead me on, make a fool of me…you must be very proud of yourself, Mr. Scott."

"Tilford!"

"What?"

"The correct name is Peter Scott Tilford!"

"Oh!"

"Cassie, don't be mad, please? Please?" He leaned over her as she turned away. "I had to do it to win Eric over. Don't you see? If I'd come barging into town announcing who I was, then Eric would've disappeared from New Beginnings completely. You have to understand, I wasn't out to fool anyone, let alone you! I've come to love attending New Beginnings. Please forgive me?"

He'd never begged for understanding before, from anyone. Something in his tone must have touched her, because she glanced up at him, tears in her eyes. "*Please* forgive me?" he added.

"Okay…." she said slowly.

"I just want lots of time to get to know Eric before we have to bring money into the conversation. Money makes people act funny."

"I suppose so," she admitted. "I imagine you'll get lots of time to talk with Eric down at the lake."

"Yeah, I suppose. But that's next month," he complained. "Let's talk about vacations. Your summer is free, right? How about going to Europe with me?"

"To Europe? With you?" Cassie said in surprise, thinking rapidly. "Oh, I guess. But I think I'll ask Maggie Wegland to go with me as a, um, companion. Is that all right?"

"That'll be nice. The more the merrier." He didn't hesitate a second. "Do I know Maggie?"

"I don't think so. She comes to New Beginnings, but she doesn't hang around after the meetings. You've seen her, though. She's very tall, almost as tall as you. And skinny. She has a couple of grown kids. They no longer live with her. She's a good friend, like Pam Lawson."

"Hmm…I think I've seen her at the meetings. So, you think you'll be ready to go in a week or ten days?"

"So soon? How come?"

"I have to be in Paris by the thirtieth. A big meeting with a South American banker."

"Well, Maggie and I'll be ready to go. Oh! I'll have to get a passport. She already has hers. She was planning a European trip this summer already."

Peter nodded. "I'll set Tony, my assistant, to expedite the passport matter."

A bit overwhelmed, all she could say was, "Thank you, Peter. That would be wonderful."

On the appointed day, Cassie picked up Maggie and drove them to Lee's Summit, where they met Peter. He led them to his private plane, introducing them to the pilot.

After about an hour they cleared the runway and climbed quickly. "You ladies all right back there?" Peter inquired.

"Yeah, but I left my stomach back at the airport," stated Maggie. "How long is the flight, anyway?"

"We'll land in New York in about three hours, and rest up. Then we'll take a commercial flight to Paris."

She nodded.

Cassie hadn't known what to expect. But as Peter had promised, they'd made a stopover in New York, then six hours later, Peter announced their arrival in Paris.

Maggie and Cassie tried to haul their own bags, but two assistants of Peter's wouldn't let them. They headed toward his limousine, but Peter lagged behind, talking to two men who had been there to meet them. Before they could get very far, Peter called, "Wait up, ladies. Are you hungry? I thought we'd eat before going to the apartment."

"Sure! Sounds great." Now that she thought about it, Cassie *was* hungry. She hadn't eaten since that morning. Was she taking on Peter's habits? she mused.

Soon they arrived at an expensive apartment building, near a church, in a well-to-do part of the city. The building was tall, and had a wonderful view of the Eiffel Tower. Cassie was excited by the thought of all the streets and sights she wanted to see. Peter would be in business meetings all day tomorrow, and she was glad Maggie had agreed to come with her.

The apartment, which was on the top floor, was furnished with expensive pieces, which Maggie oohed and aahed over, and Cassie simply studied, then said, "Very nice."

"I inherited most of the furnishings from my father," Peter offered. "But a few pieces I bought for myself. Here, this small table is one." He pointed to a tiny three-tiered tea table sitting next to a long white sofa.

Later, in their bedroom, Cassie and Maggie pored over a map of the city, spotlighting the sights they wanted to see. Peter knocked and came into their room without ceremony. "I've instructed Tony to accompany you about the city. To escort you to see the sights." For protection, he privately thought.

"That's very kind of you. Won't Tony get bored?" Cassie asked.

"He doesn't, honestly. He's a regular

tourist, anywhere we go, and loves to show off his knowledge. Besides, I pay him too much for him to get bored."

"All right, then," said Maggie.

"What time will you be through with your meetings?" asked Cassie. "Will you join us at any time?"

"I should be through by three."

"Three? Then we can have high tea, I suppose."

"High tea in France? You are mistaking our location. Next week, while we're in England, if you please. But if you want, I'll meet you for an espresso. I'll order it for here, if you don't mind. I am usually worn out by the South Americans in meetings."

"Yes, that'll be fine." said Cassie, after a glance at Maggie. "Till three?"

That set their week. Each day Cassie and Maggie found a new tourist spot or an ancient church, which fascinated Cassie, to visit, while Peter met with his business associates. They walked everywhere, then met back at Peter's flat after three o'clock, and had an espresso before deciding what they would do during the evening.

One morning they happened into a fabric shop, and Cassie and Maggie were both in awe over the beauty of the fabrics they found. Peter's meeting had been canceled, and he'd joined them on their shopping spree.

"This lovely deep pink is just what I need for my front room," Cassie whispered.

"But it's too costly."

"Can't you substitute something else?" Maggie suggested.

"I guess I'll have to, since this is out of my price range."

"I'll help you pick out something when we get home, if you want me to," Maggie offered. "Shopping around can be fun, if you know where to shop."

"Okay. I'll call on you when we get home, then." Cassie tucked the idea away in the back of her mind. She'd only begun to think of what she was going to do with her living room and how she was going to change it. She'd welcome any ideas Maggie could come up with.

After a week in Paris, they went to England, exchanging their afternoon espressos for high tea. After a week, on a Tuesday, Peter announced he needed to be in Rome in a couple of days, startling Maggie and Cassie with his sudden plans. Why was Peter needed in Rome at the drop of a hat?

"Perhaps we should just go home. Or stay in London to wait for you," Cassie offered.

"Nonsense," Peter replied. "I've gotten used to seeing you two at the end of my day." He turned to Cassie. "Aren't you glad to see that I eat? You're a good influence on me." He smiled.

Cassie finally agreed, and Peter made arrangements. Rome was exciting, even though their visit was only for a couple of days. Tony took them sightseeing, walking everywhere as usual. One afternoon, Peter surprised them and joined them as they toured. He mentioned that they'd be headed to Holland soon, to an organ factory to choose one for their church back home.

That night, Cassie sat straight up in bed and gasped. "I can't get a handle on all this. Peter really is wealthy, isn't he?" she asked Maggie.

"I guess he is. He seems to be one of the wealthiest men in the world. Why, last month *Newsweek* did a piece on him."

"Really? Why didn't we see it?"

"Peter wanted to keep his identity a secret, I suppose," Maggie replied. "Boy, wait till I tell Pam about the places we've seen. And the people I work with."

Cassie hadn't a single friend she could tell.

By now, Cassie and Maggie were

thoroughly entranced with the churches of Europe, and wanted to see those of Holland, as well. When they flew into the airport in Holland, Maggie had dozens of questions. How long had the organ company been in business? How many did they make? Were there different types of organs?

Peter stayed close to Cassie as they all toured the plant. He asked several more questions, then ordered an organ, one that had special pipes to play the most complicated music. One that needed a tuner to attend to it after it was properly installed.

"Pastor Mike and Mr. and Mrs. Hostetter will be very surprised over this," remarked Cassie. She turned as she spoke to find Peter standing near. His face was only inches from hers. They stared at each other for a long moment, and Cassie felt she was lost in his blue, blue eyes.

"Yes, but pleased, I think," Maggie

finally replied. Then she cleared her throat. "Are you sure you can afford it, Peter?"

He shrugged, still staring at Cassie. "If *I* can't, nobody can."

They arranged for it to be shipped back home, arriving in a month's time. They would be back in the U.S. long before it arrived, thought Cassie. But who did they have in their congregation who could play a complicated pipe organ? She thought to e-mail Pastor Mike so that he would be on the lookout for an accomplished player.

No matter how rich he was, Peter couldn't buy them an organ player, too.

Chapter Thirteen

They all arrived home from Europe without incident. Cassie was surprised by how glad she was to see her home; the house looked solid and secure in the old neighborhood.

"I'll have to cut the grass before heading down to the lake property the day after tomorrow," she remarked to Peter.

"Why don't you let me do that, Cassie?" Peter asked as they parked in front of the house. She didn't answer.

"Why would you want to?" she wondered aloud a moment later. He unloaded her suitcases, then carried them up the concrete stairs to her front door.

"I need the exercise," he said as he was leaving.

"You'll get plenty of that down at the lake," she replied. "Peter, I want to thank you for the wonderful trip to Europe. Neither Maggie nor I will ever forget it."

"I'm glad you could come, Cassie. I'll be going again in a few weeks." Standing in the front room, he slid his arms around her and drew her close, kissing her lightly. The picture of her father and mother stared down at them from the mantel. "Perhaps you can come with me again."

"Perhaps I will," she answered, feeling guilty for wanting to go with him. Her father's face seemed positively grim. She looked up into Peter's face, earnest and sober, but pleasant. He really wanted her to come? He didn't think of her as a nuisance?

"I've got to go, now, hon," he said as

he placed a quick kiss on her mouth. "But I'll be in touch."

"Don't forget, I'll see you Thursday, when we go to the lake."

"Yes, you will." He turned on the walk to glance back at her, saluting her. "I'll be there."

Peter thought of his brother. He would be at the lake, too. He planned to talk to Eric for hours, in hopes of cementing their relationship.

"There'll be enough work to go around, down at the lake."

"True. But I hope there'll be some fun, too."

"Fun? I'm sure there will be enough."

"Good. I'll see you on Thursday, then." As usual, he was reluctant to leave Cassie. It didn't seem right. He couldn't put a finger on it, but he always felt peaceful in her presence.

That was worth a whole mountain. He hesitated before he climbed back into the car. Should he ask her to marry him again? She seemed to take offense when he did before. How could he make her see that he meant it?

He'd have opportunity down at the lake, he told himself.

Cassie entered her house again and walked from room to room, inspecting it thoroughly. It needed redecorating badly. She felt her father's presence in the rooms. Cassie sighed, remember his fussing, his complaining, his sniping comments. This was his house, his and her mother's.

She sighed again. She should sell the house and buy one of those town houses she and Peter had looked at in the spring. She'd rather liked the ones in Independence, near the square. Though the square was no longer a shopping center, it had enough activity to interest her.

She'd never lived anywhere else but this house. What would it be like living in a town house? She thought of all the places in Europe she and Maggie had seen. Peter's apartment in Paris was positively tiny. She'd investigate moving as soon as she got back from the lake. It seemed like the right thing to do.

Thursday dawned bright and sunny, a great day for the long drive. She packed some old clothes for working, and drove the few miles to the church. Most of the others were there. But where was Peter?

They were about to take off when Peter came roaring up to them on his motorcycle.

"Is it all right to park my bike here in the lot?" he asked.

"Sure," Pastor Mike answered. "It'll be fine. If you feel nervous about leaving it, I can call Reverend Hostetter to pick it up and put it into his garage for the weekend."

"No, no. I should have had Tony drop me off, but he had work to do."

Pastor Mike nodded. "Okay. Shall we be off?"

They all climbed into the van. Peter sat next to her, and Cassie felt safe. She recalled their last trip down, with Lori getting injured. "How is Lori?" she remembered to ask.

"Lori is just fine," replied Pastor Mike. "Understandably, she decided to pass on joining the work crew."

"What other women are going, then?" Cassie asked.

"Oh, Gena Donaldson, and my wife, Rina. They're bringing a lot of food. I'm thinking we need all of you for the painting crew. Do any of you have any objections to that?"

"Not a one. Did the furnace and air-conditioning crew get down to fix the problems with those units?" asked Peter.

"They did. Last week, while you were gone," the pastor replied. "They put in a big new hot-water heater, too. I'm hoping all will be well with the air-conditioning. It's supposed to be hot this week."

After driving for a while, once more they approached the hill that the property sat on. "We need a name for this place," Peter said.

"I've been thinking about that. I proposed that the New Beginnings crew think about it. Someone came up with the name 'Embryo,'" Pastor Mike said.

"That isn't very appealing," stated Jason, who sat in the back of the van.

"Can you think of something else?" asked Pastor Mike.

"Hmm…" muttered Peter. "How about 'Élan'? Meaning 'spirit'?"

"Oh, that's excellent! I think that's the name," Pastor Mike exclaimed. "Do you all agree?"

Everyone did.

"Anyone hungry yet?" asked Cassie as they pulled up to the curve in the road with the slight hill that hid their new retreat. She'd packed a few sandwiches.

"Yeah," said Mark, and another voice Cassie thought was Eric.

"Okay, let's eat, then divide up into work crews. Pam, you and Maggie can work with me." Cassie wanted the two other women on her team.

They quickly devoured the sandwiches, then divided the jobs they'd planned to tackle on this first trip to the lake. Pastor Mike maneuvered his way to Rina's side as she joined Charlie's team, working on the outside deck. Rina seemed a little distant, but Cassie shrugged it off. Peter said he'd work with Eric, clearing the grounds. Cassie, alone, prepared her paintbrushes, then set to work on the front of the house.

Wide stroking made the painting go faster. The sun shone brightly until it settled behind the hills. "Let's go for a boat ride," said Peter. "Wow, you've made a lot of progress! C'mon, Cassie, you've worked enough for one day."

"All right. Help me clean up." Cassie had paint all over herself, but the front of the house looked refreshingly white.

She poured turpentine over the brushes, and a cloth to clean windows and splashes of paint where there shouldn't be, then swiped at her arms and hands. Soon every brush was clean, and every can of paint was efficiently tucked away beside the house. Then she ran down to the dock.

Charlie was there standing beside a huge motorboat. Climbing into it, Eric muttered something about safety, and handed each of them a life vest. They struggled to put them on, and Peter suddenly appeared to help Cassie buckle hers up the front.

Charlie eased the motor into full swing, and they were off. He took them into the main channel of the lake, where other boats were running down the lake.

Peter sat beside Cassie, reaching for her hand. She welcomed it, his fingers feeling secure and warm after the long day of holding only a paint brush.

They made a wide path along the shore, admiring the places they saw. "I like those swings, under those trees," remarked Cassie. "But it takes years for trees to grow like that."

Eric answered, "Yeah, but we have trees in the woods that we might find to support swings, if you want them. We could even make a garden there, if you want. There's enough open ground to plant one."

"That's an idea to pursue," Cassie answered. She leaned back and enjoyed the breeze created by the boat's movement. Her hair was tossed behind her.

Peter watched the peaceful expression on her face. She seemed perfectly content.

What was it about Cassie that made him so happy? Sometimes he yearned to hold her in his arms, for always—to hold her and never let her go.

As they neared the rotting dock that was attached to their place, he let go, for just a moment. He caught her in his arms, kissing her tenderly, with all the emotions that had built over the last weeks.

Could he be falling in love with her?

Chapter Fourteen

After telling Cassie he wanted some time alone with Eric, Cassie arranged to be elsewhere as the evening sun shone over the hills. Peter made his way over to Eric, who was sitting at the dock.

"Hi, Eric."

"Hi, Peter."

"Mind if I sit with you a while?"

"Why would I mind, when it was you who donated this place to New Beginnings?"

Startled at Eric's correct guess, Peter asked, "Why would you say a thing like that? The place was given anonymously."

"It's what our father would've done. I'm not wrong, am I?"

It was a long moment as Peter mulled over his answer. If he didn't answer honestly, Eric would always question other answers he gave. "No. You're not wrong. And yes, our dad would've done something like buying this place as a retreat for New Beginnings. But New Beginnings has come to mean a lot to me personally, too. I wanted the organization to have it."

"What has New Beginnings meant to you, Peter?"

"Oh, something to believe in, besides what my money can buy. A savior, someone I'd never really known before."

"That's nice. Do you know Him— Jesus—now?"

"I think I do. Do you, Eric?"

"Certainly. The creation causes me to believe in a creator. This whole place couldn't have come into existence without God. He made all the animals, the little ones. And when one of them needs my help, I can't help not giving it."

"I understand. You know, our dad didn't want to lose contact with you. But your mom—"

"I know, I know! You don't have to say more. I forgive him, as I've forgiven my mom…that's what all the Biblical teachings are about. God loves and forgives, so we must, as well."

"Dad left you a sizeable inheritance. I've kept it in a money market fund for you. You can draw on it at any time. You can go to college now, if you want to. To study veterinary medicine."

"I guess. I'll have to think about it all."

"Yes, I suppose so. You don't want to do anything foolish, do you?"

"No. I've never had much money. But now I can think of a dozen ways to spend it. There's some land I want to buy…."

Suddenly, a call came from the house. "Supper. Supper, guys!"

"Let's go," exclaimed Eric as he climbed to his feet. "I'm starved."

"Me, too," Peter added.

As the two men walked into the house, Peter said, "Something smells great! Cassie, you'd make a good mom, I'm thinking. Are you sure you won't marry me?"

Cassie ducked her head while a flush rose to her cheeks.

"When you get serious about that question, then I'll give you a serious answer."

Cassie was thoughtful throughout dinner, listening to Peter and Eric trade stories of their childhood. "Even though he was a lousy dad, he was proud of his sons," Peter remarked. "He was certainly proud of you, Eric."

"I suppose so," Eric replied, though his tone implicated he would be loath to trust his dad.

Peter lay down his fork, folded his hands, and stared at his brother. "Tilford Enterprises could use a man like you. Are you sure you don't want a job?"

Eric shook his head. "Thanks for the offer, but my life is too full as it is. Working for you, I'd have no time to look after my animals."

Peter nodded in understanding. "Well, keep the offer in mind. You never know, you might want it in future."

Peter's head looked Cassie's way. "And you keep my offer in mind, as well, please, Cassie? I don't want to lose you to someone else, just because I didn't ask you at the right moment. I'm too busy to worry about it right now."

"That's just the trouble, Peter. You'd be so busy that you'd take me for granted. You'd work long hours and ignore me completely."

"Did I do that in Europe?"

"No, but I expect after a time you'd forget about me. You'd expect me to entertain myself and carry on without you. Apologies wouldn't make everything all right, you know. Or roses."

"That's just it!" Peter exclaimed. "I'd want you to keep me from working too much."

"And how would I do that, if you're determined to work?"

"I think you could make me change my ways."

"This discussion has gone on long enough," Cassie stated. "I have a kitchen to clean and you guys can get lost."

"Aw, Cassie," Peter protested, chuckling.

Cassie went to clean up, then just as she had a dishpan full of warm suds, Peter knocked at the kitchen door. "I came to help you with the dishes," he announced.

"You?"

"Yes, me, sweetheart. Why not?"

"I don't know. I just don't picture you doing something so—so mundane."

"You'll see." He headed toward the sink. "I can be domestic when I want to be."

"Then dry," she pronounced, handing him a dish towel.

He took it and silently reached for a clean dish, drying with too little effort. He placed the dish onto the table to be put away later. Cassie washed and Peter dried, until they completed the job.

As he performed his task, Peter's mind was focused on business. Cassie recognized the faraway look in his eyes but said nothing. When he'd spent almost ten minutes on the last dish, she pulled it from his hands, setting it on the table beside the other dishes.

"That's it, Peter."

"What's it?"

"That's all of the dishes."

"Oh." He glanced around and saw that everything was finished. He fluffed out his dish towel and hung it over the back of a chair. "Now what?" he asked Cassie.

"Now your time is your own."

"Then I'll say good night. I have some work to do."

"That's what I thought," she murmured, and turned away to hide her thoughts while her heart dipped.

"What's that supposed to mean?" he asked.

"Nothing. I meant you'd always be working, leaving me to find my own amusement."

"Oh, that again."

"Yes, *that* again." She wouldn't allow him to get under her skin.

But he'd done that already.

Well, she'd learn to protect herself better, wouldn't she?

After spending time at the lodge, several days went by, and Cassie didn't hear from Peter. She wondered where he was, how he was. She busied herself with housework and shopping. The refrigerator was full of uneaten food.

And she baked, even though the days were hot.

She baked banana bread, oatmeal cake and chocolate chip cookies. Thinking of her next classroom of children, she carefully placed each in the freezer, ready to pull out whenever she needed them.

She was in the middle of breaking eggs when the phone rang. She hurriedly set aside the eggs, wiped her hands on a towel, then grabbed the wall phone.

"Cassie?" It was Peter.

"Oh, hi, Peter."

"What are you doing."

"I'm baking."

"What? In this heat? Well, you want to go for a ride? On the motorcycle?" he asked.

"Sure. When?"

"Now. In about ten minutes. I'm getting close to where you live. Be ready, okay?"

Cassie glanced at her messy kitchen. "Okay. I'll be ready."

Cassie hung up and spent five of her precious ten minutes hurriedly putting away the ingredients that needed refrigeration, then rushed upstairs to throw her jeans on.

She had one foot in, when she heard the roar of his bike. "Oh, no. Please, not yet!" she moaned as she caught her foot in the pants and sat down suddenly on the bed.

She untangled her foot as she heard Peter enter the house, calling her name at the top of his voice.

"I'll be right there. Why are you in such a hurry about, anyway?"

"Pastor Mike wants us to meet with his committee this morning about the pipe organ. They want to know who will be coming to install it!"

"Didn't you tell them the company will send someone who knows how it should be installed?" she said, lowering her voice as she came down the stairs in her ragged jeans and pink T-shirt.

"Yeah," Peter answered, his eyes admiring her now slender figure. She'd walked so much in Europe, she'd lost some weight. "But there are a couple of committee members who want reassurance, Pastor Mike says. He says they're always a pain to deal with."

"Why don't we take them some of the cookies I just baked to sweeten them up?" she asked.

"Now, there's an idea…." Peter said.

"Okay. Just let me get them."

A tin filled with cookies clutched to her body, she rode with Peter to meet with the committee. They met in the church office, cramped but with the fragrance of freshly baked cookies teasing their noses.

"These are very good, Cassie," remarked elderly Mr. Tidewater. "My missus used to bake these when our children were small. Now her arthritis is so bad she doesn't cook or bake at all."

"That's too bad, Mr. Tidewater. Have

some more." Cassie passed her tin of cookies around again.

"They are quite delicious," said Mrs. Berry. "Now about this pipe organ. Where are we to put it? Did anyone think of that? And who's going to play it?"

"I think it will have to go into the balcony," said Pastor Mike.

"What if it's too big for the space?" asked Mr. Tidewater. "And who can we get to play?"

"Let's cross one bridge at a time," the pastor said, calming the fitful questions. "Many churches have their organs in their balconies and there's plenty of space there. We might have to have some new wiring, but that's not out of the question. We have electricians in our congregation who can see to that. In fact, I've called Charlie. He'll inspect it all, and figure out the wiring we need. Chris can inspect the balcony floor to make sure it's strong enough to hold the organ."

"All that's already been done?" asked Mrs. Berry.

"Yes, I made the calls as soon as I heard an organ was purchased," Pastor Mike said, casting a glance at Peter.

"When is the organ being delivered?" Mr. Tidewater asked.

"In a month." Cassie spoke up. "I—rather, we—toured the factory, and chose the organ. It's beautiful, that's all, just beautiful, made of mahogany with ivory keys. Can Miss Adams play it?" She mentioned the woman who played the church piano. "Can't she take a stab at it?"

"I don't think so, dear," answered Mrs. Berry. "We'll have to find someone besides Janie Adams to play an organ."

"All right. We'll advertise for a organist," said Pastor Mike. "Now, if that's all we have to take care of, let's visit the balcony."

One by one, they all climbed the steep stairs to the balcony. The wood railing was smooth with all the hands that had run by it over time. Cassie eyed the space doubtfully. But Peter seemed to think it was all right.

"Does someone have a tape measure?" asked Mrs. Berry.

"I do," announced Peter. He pulled the thing out of his pocket and handed one end of it to Pastor Mike. "Hold this," he instructed. "And stand in front of that window."

Pastor Mike did as he was told. Then Peter unreeled the tape measure and stepped backward until he reached the opposite wall. "It'll fit," he said, then under his breath, "just barely. Might have to make some adjustments with these railings, Pastor."

"We'll have to make adjustments, all right, but it will be with the pipes, I think," the pastor replied.

"Can't we put some of them on a shelf into the wall?" asked Mr. Tidewater.

"That's a wonderful idea," remarked Mrs. Berry.

"Then that's what we'll do. It'll be terrific," said Mr. Tidewater. Cassie's regard for the old man immediately went up a notch. Mr. Tidewater was a visionary. "The church will gain fame and give glory to the Lord!"

"That is if we can find an organist," murmured Mrs. Berry. Since all were satisfied, at least for the moment, they quickly ended the meeting, and left the church. In the parking lot, as Cassie climbed on the back of the cycle, she sighed.

"What's the matter, hon?" asked Peter.

"I don't know. I guess I can hardly visualize the organ up in the balcony. There's hardly room enough for all the congregation to sit without the balcony for overflow worshippers now. Where are we going to put everybody?"

"Maybe it's time to build a new building," Peter suggested.

"You think?" Cassie replied, and let the matter drop.

"I can't give a whole new building to the church, Cassie. But I'd be glad to help."

"I wouldn't expect you to give a whole new building, Peter. It's enough that you gave that beautiful instrument."

"Well, let's get going. I'm starved, as usual. Have you buckled your seat belt?"

"Sure."

"I instructed Tony to secure us a reservation at Lisa and Ethan's restaurant. Ethan promised to play at nine. We want to be there for that."

"Oh, yes, I love it when Ethan plays."

Cassie slid her arms tightly around Peter, and they headed off. She closed her eyes while they were traveling, something she'd never told Peter. Judging the right amount of time, she opened them when they slowed, reaching Independence Square. She directed Peter down a couple of blocks to the restaurant.

Lisa met them at the door, looking

gorgeous in a navy linen sheath dress, then led them to a table in the corner. The place was full and the noise level was high. She could hardly hear Lisa.

"How are your kids?" she asked Lisa.

"Oh, they're fine. You might see them running about, later. We couldn't get a sitter for the night, so we brought them down. But they're pretty well-behaved."

"That's nice," Cassie said.

When the time came, Ethan stepped out and the room quieted. He strummed a bit on his guitar, then first one child then another came out and stood beside him. He led them in a rollicking version of "Old MacDonald." One voice stood out from the group, and he asked the child to sing. The child, a little boy, began to sing. Ethan joined at the chorus.

Noticing a melancholy look on Peter's face, Cassie reached across the table to take his hand. "Do you miss your son very badly, Peter?"

"Yes, I miss him dreadfully. But I confess, I never had the closeness that those children have with their father. I mourn that empty time now. And I wished I'd had more children."

Cassie grew quiet. What could she say to bring him comfort?

Cassie thought of all her fifth-graders. They served a purpose in her life, certainly. She had all the children she liked from September to June. But she'd often wanted, in her younger days, to marry and have children of her own.

Now it was too late. She'd never have a child of her own. A deep sadness crept over her, and she squeezed Peter's hand in real empathy.

With the performance ended, their food came. But they were both very quiet during their meal.

Later, saying good-night at her door, Peter whispered as he lingered, "You're right, Cassie. You're helping me change that day by day. Thank you." He kissed her softly, then rode off into the night on his bike.

The next week, another group of workers made the trip down to the lake. There was plenty to still be done to the lodge. Cassie came prepared to work—alone. Peter was in New York again—working.

Pastor Mike drove carefully through the rain. It wasn't raining hard, simply a gentle rain. Cassie wasn't disturbed by it; it would give her a chance to see the lake property in inclement weather.

Later on, she sat on the long sofa and stared out the window for quite a time, thinking. Children. She did long for a child of her own.

She thought of Mrs. Martinez, with too many children. It wasn't fair, she silently wailed....

The next day the weather cleared nicely, so Cassie got out her paint and brushes. The front bedroom of the cabin needed a fresh coat of lilac paint. She opened the window to let the air flow.

She heard a lot of hammering going on, and at noon, when she stopped long enough to go down to the kitchen, she discovered a new cabinet over the stove in the kitchen.

Cassie was glad she hadn't signed up to teach summer school this year. She had plenty to keep her busy with the current activities in New Beginnings.

The cabin crew worked hard until they left at dawn Sunday morning, early enough to be back for services.

"If you don't want to make me look bad to Pastor Hostetter," said Pastor Mike, "you'll hurry and come to the morning worship service."

"I'll be there," stated Cassie. She had run into her student Rico in the supermarket last week. He'd promised her he'd be at services this morning and she wanted to see if he was there.

At home, hurrying along, Cassie threw on an old white dress and some sandals and went to church. Sure enough, Rico was standing outside, visiting with other children about his own age when she drove by, looking for a place to park.

"You kept your promise, Rico," she remarked when she came closer. "I love men who keep their promises."

"I sure did, Miss Manning." He puffed out his chest.

"How's your mother? Is she well?"

"Nah. She has morning sickness. It's the same as last time. It must be a boy."

"Your mother is going to have another baby?" Cassie gasped. She felt so sorry for Mrs. Martinez. Six kids in as many years was a problem to raise.

"Yeah. What else is new?"

"Say, would you like to go to the Nelson Art Museum? I'll be going this Friday. It's free on Fridays." At his grimace she added, "I promise you'll *love* the museum." Thinking to take him for an outing, she also thought to relieve his mother for an afternoon.

"I guess so. Can my two sisters come, too?"

"Why not?"

"Okay, great! What time?"

She suggested a time to pick up the children. On Friday morning, she got a call from Peter. He was in New York. She told him, "I'm going to the art museum today with some former students of mine."

"Good. Now you'll stay out of trouble," he joked.

"I always stay out of trouble."

"I don't know... You won't run off with your latest beau, will you?"

"Since you're my latest beau, you know the answer to that."

"Okay, that gives me hope. I'll call you in the morning."

"I'll look forward to it."

Chapter Fifteen

At the agreed-upon time, she drove up to Rico's house and picked up Rico and his sisters, Carlotta and Josie. The girls sat primly on either side of Rico.

At the museum, she parked the car on the street, and they walked to the front of the museum. She nodded to the guard as she went through.

First they looked at the Chinese art. Then they walked through the sculpture. Then they viewed the paintings. Each was fascinating. A nearby tour guide discussed the brush strokes and Cassie listened unashamedly, shushing the kids so that she could hear. She thought of all the museums she'd seen in Europe, and wondered if she'd ever tire of seeing more paintings.

But she discovered she missed Peter, because she realized she'd never brought him to her hometown museum. They went through the museum until Josie complained she was getting hungry. Cassie looked at her watch. Oh, my goodness, she thought. It was five-thirty. No wonder Josie was hungry!

Time for high tea, Cassie thought. Unfortunately, here in America, there was no such thing.

"Okay. We've had enough of this museum. Let's walk back through."

It seemed a long way back out of the museum and then back to the car, but they dragged on. When they finally got into the old car, Rico asked, "Can we come back sometime?"

"Of course we can. Did you like it?"

"I want to paint like one of those painters," stated Carlotta.

"Me, too," chimed in Rico.

"Perhaps you can take private art lessons. I'll have to find a teacher, I suppose."

Cassie wondered if her friend from school, Donna Withers, would be willing to teach private art lessons to the kids without pay.

When she dropped the kids off at their house, it was with ice-cream cones in hand. They'd had a marvelous afternoon, and she didn't regret a moment of it. But it was a lot more difficult seeing a museum here than seeing a museum, in say, Paris, with Tony looking after everything. She sighed for the easiness of her European days.

Peter called again. Oh, no! He wasn't going to be back for another month, he said. When Cassie hung up the phone, she went to the kitchen and made a sandwich.

She gazed at the beautiful fabric he'd sent her. The Paris store had told her the fabric was out of stock, when she asked. But here it was….

It would go a long way toward her home's renovation.

A month went by. She lined out all the bills to be paid on the kitchen table, and stared at them. She could pay the utilities; the doctor and funeral costs she still owed. She could pay only half of that. Where could she earn a little extra money?

She thought of asking Lisa if they needed help at the restaurant, but she was really too clumsy. She'd have to read the help wanted ads.

When she picked up her copy of the day's paper, it was there in black and white. The orchards! They needed pickers. And Lisa and Ethan had said they needed a babysitter. Those were definite possibilities.

Early the next morning, she made arrangements to pick peaches, and she called Lisa at the restaurant.

Lisa was overjoyed at her offer. "Are you sure? I can use you every night, if you're free."

"I won't be free every night, but I'll be glad to start tonight," Cassie explained.

Peter wasn't as enthusiastic about her working, when he called. He especially objected to the babysitting.

"In any case, I'll be in New York," Peter replied. Provoking man! He didn't seem a bit upset that they were spending less and less time together.

She waited for Peter to call her. He seemed to stay in New York a long time. But the days crawled by without the phone ringing. Cassie cleaned the living room within an inch of scrubbing the paint off. She looked again at the material Peter had sent, hanging it against the windows. It'd look gorgeous, but then she'd need a new couch and chairs, which she couldn't buy until the last hospital bill was paid.

Her first day of peach picking proved to be one of hard work and sweat. She hadn't imagined her arms would be so tired. Yet as she set her last bushel of the day on the truck, she vowed to stick it out. She could rest tonight.

Getting ready to go over to Lisa and Ethan's house, she rummaged in her medicine cabinet for some aloe vera to put on her sunburned skin. That would teach her to wear sunblock, she vowed.

Lisa was glad to see her. The children all jumped around her, and she discovered they wanted to see a Disney cartoon. Her next hour was relaxed as the children were glued to the TV, and they ate the pizza Lisa had left them for dinner. Cassie didn't eat much. She was too tired for much besides holding little Ceceily on her lap while the child ate and watched *Bambi*.

At almost eleven, Lisa and Ethan

stumbled in from their restaurant, tired and ready for bed. Cassie said good-night and went home. The evening hadn't been too bad.

The phone rang just as she climbed into bed.

"Hello?"

"Cassie? You're finally home. Where have you been? I've called you three times today."

"I've been babysitting, Peter. I'm earning extra money this summer. I should've taken a summer school-teacher's job, but I didn't. So I'm baby-sitting in the evenings for Ethan and Lisa. And picking peaches in the daytime."

"Peaches?"

"Yes, there are peach and apple or-chards in the middle of northern Missouri, didn't you know? And wineries down south, in the middle of the state."

"Really? No, I didn't know that about Missouri. Giving California a run for its money, huh? We'll have to visit those places. Especially the apple orchards. I love apples."

"All right, we can go to one of those pick-your-own orchards. You're on. And I'd like to bring along some children, too, if I may?"

"Oh, Cassie. I can't see taking children with us. They'll get in the way, won't they?"

"But you'll like these kids," Cassie explained. "Rico is very smart, and learns quickly. I don't know his sisters very well, but Carlotta likes art, and Josie wants to be a dancer."

There was a hesitation before he said, "Sure, why not?"

"When will you be back in town?" she asked.

"Soon. I'm trying to wrap up some business now. I'll let you know."

"All right, you do that. Good night."

"Good night, sweetheart. Sleep well."

She quickly hung the receiver in its cradle. Peter was miffed because she wanted to take along some children on their adventures? She thought of Rico and his sisters, imagining them high in an apple tree. She laughed aloud. Then she giggled when her imagination sent Peter up the tree with them.

Early Saturday morning, Peter phoned again. He was in town. "Eric would like to go fruit picking with us," he said.

"Okay. We'll have a real party."

Cassie set a time with Peter. She picked up Rico and his sisters, and had them waiting at her house before Peter arrived.

"Is he your boyfriend?" asked Rico when Peter climbed out of the car in front of her house. Rico glared at Peter as he was coming up the walk, and his sisters tried to shush him.

"Yes. Is that all right with you?" Cassie answered the boy. Was Rico jealous?

"I don't know," Rico said with a frown. "I don't know him, do I?"

"This is your chance to get acquainted," Cassie said.

The day proved to be hot and humid. The children were directed to pick with an adult, something which they resented. But they soon settled down to their own territory, and began to pick. "Pick the best, ripest peaches you can find," Cassie instructed. "No, not off the ground, unless they're not bruised." She caught Jolie just before she was about to put one in her basket.

Rico stuck by Cassie's side. They climbed high on a ladder in the tree, holding their baskets tightly. Cassie rested her basket in a crook in the tree, and reached for a big peach. She planned on baking several pies tonight, and would then put them in the freezer. When the teachers had their get-togethers in the fall, she'd pull out one of her pies.

She'd have enough for a bit of jam, too. The children would have enough to take home, as well. She glanced at Rico.

He had already filled his basket about halfway.

At the end of the morning, she called a halt. They stood in line at the weigh station to pay. Then Rico stated that he was hungry.

"How can you be, with juice all over your mouth?" Cassie asked, laughing. She suspected he'd eaten his share of the juicy fruit, and hoped that doing so hadn't ruined his taste for peaches.

"Well, let's get these baskets weighed, and we'll see about lunch," she told him.

"Are we expected to take these little moppets to lunch, too?" Peter whispered in her ear.

"I packed sandwiches for all of us," she whispered back with a smile.

"You did? What have you packed for me? Peanut butter and jelly?"

"Can you buy us some drinks, Peter?"

"I suppose so." Since they were next up in line, he pulled his wallet free from his pocket.

"Children, why don't you find us a picnic table?"

They left their baskets on the ground beside her, and ran toward the picnic tables a few yards away. Eric started laughing.

"Can you take care of my peaches, too?" he asked, and raced after the children. He swooped up Rico and whirled him around. When they stopped, Eric sat Rico's feet on the ground, but Rico staggered about like he was dizzy.

"Swing me, swing me," begged the girls.

"He's good with the kids," Peter murmured in Cassie's ear as he paid for the peaches.

He purchased enough soft drinks for everyone, then carried his tray toward the picnic table. Cassie grabbed her small cooler, packed with sandwiches, and laid them out. Some were indeed peanut butter and jelly. The kids grabbed them up as eagerly as they did the ham and cheese, and chicken salad.

Peter just shook his head at the kid's appetites, then went to the check-out stand and bought fruit turnovers for all. "Thanks, Peter. You're a good sport."

"Remember that, will you?" he answered.

They packed up and went home, dropping the kids off, happy and worn out. They left a basket of peaches with a very grateful Mrs. Martinez. Eric left them at the church corner.

Peter lay down on her sofa. This was getting to be a habit, Cassie thought. Cassie watched his tired eyes gently close. Then going to her knees on the floor beside him, she traced the lines in his face with her finger. Though he had them, it didn't take away from his good looks. She merely thought he worked too hard.

He slept for more than an hour. When he woke, he seemed surprised that he'd slept. Refreshed, Peter suggested a movie after dinner. Cassie was agreeable. They chose one, way on the north side of town.

"Did we look at town houses up this way?" asked Peter.

"No. We never got this far," Cassie told him.

"Hmm…there's lots of land left up here for development, isn't there?" Peter went very quiet.

Cassie wondered what he was thinking.

"Eric seemed to have a good time today," she remarked. "And since you like apples, we could do this again when the apples are ripe."

"Only if you promise me you'll bake me an apple pie."

"Oh, there'll be pie enough. I might ask Lisa if Ethan can use them in his kitchen."

"That's an idea. Work for Lisa and Ethan."

"I have been. I've been babysitting."

"You've been what?"

"That's right. I told you about it, remember? I wanted to pay off my father's funeral expenses before school started, so I'm babysitting."

"How much does it pay?"

"Not very much, but I love being with the kids. And there are perks. Like not being so lonely. You've been gone a long time, Peter."

"I'm sorry. But I'm back now." He paused for a moment, then said, "We still have to go down to the lodge and work, right?"

"Yes, we do," she replied. "There are some final touches to be done. Pastor Mike thinks we can use it by the fall, for retreats."

"Let's go down next weekend."

"Yes, let's."

"And we still have to research for a place for me to live. I'm getting awfully tired of living in a motel when I'm in town. I don't suppose you'd rent a room to me, would you?"

A quick glance at her told him his answer.

"We'll find you a place, don't worry," she said.

He sighed. "Okay. How about if I pick you up after lunch on Wednesday? Then we can look at town houses in the afternoon, and go on to the Wednesday evening service."

"Yes, that sounds good."

Peter left. She took her peaches into the kitchen and began to wash them. She loved having the fresh fruit, and thought about making pies for the restaurant.

It would be one more way to earn money.

Chapter Sixteen

At the lodge, Cassie carefully painted a border around the lilac room. It was really pretty, she thought. She should do something like it for her room at home. Better yet, why not take the larger front bedroom that used to be her parents' bedroom, and paint it for herself?

Would it be too odd? Sleeping in her parents' room? She thought about that. Yeah, she thought it would be. But if she changed it all about? It was worth a try.

She carefully put the paint and everything else away, and went downstairs to find Peter and the others who'd come for the weekend. Pam, on a rare week-end away from her boys, was busy var-nishing the kitchen cabinets.

"We'll be ready to use this place by Labor Day," said Pastor Mike. "You folks have really worked hard getting this place in shape. I really thank you."

"I, for one, really thank you, Pastor Mike," said Charlie. "This has been the most fun I've had since I was a teen."

"It's been a lot of fun for me, too," agreed Chris.

"Let's go for a walk before dinner, and see what Eric has been up to," Peter whispered in Cassie's ear.

"All right," Cassie agreed.

They left the house and strolled down to the repaired boat dock. They wandered about a bit, then, hand in hand, took the path along the shore, walking in front of other houses. They returned by way of the pathway that Eric had cleared, through tall trees and flowers he'd planted along the borders.

"I must remember to tell Eric how lovely his pathway is," Cassie said.

"Yes, I'm finding my brother is quite talented in ways I never was," Peter remarked.

"That's often the case," said Cassie. "You'd think kids from the same parents would have the same interests in life, but they can be quite different."

"Eric and I have different mothers," Peter reminded her. "Our father didn't have trouble finding wives, he just had trouble keeping them." He paused for a moment. "My record hasn't been much better. I truly wish I'd made good decisions about marriage, or rather the women I married. But, Cassie, I'm not making a poor decision about you. You're a woman of class, and faith. Your faith makes you beautiful.

"Beautiful in a way that I need. I need you, Cassie. Very much. And I love you so much. I wish we could have a family. With you, I'd be a very good father, I think. When you look at me in such a way, I know I've done something to please you."

Surprised at his utterances, she stood very still along the path, and stared at him. "Really, Peter?"

"Yes, really. Cassie, won't you say you'll marry me? I'll shrivel up and die without you."

No one was about to hear the proposal. He wasn't teasing this time. He was dead serious.

"If you put it that way, Peter, then I'd be happy to marry you. I love you with all my heart, and want a life together."

He threw back his head and yelped the loudest yelp Cassie had ever heard. "Right away?"

"If that's what you want," she replied.

They heard pounding footsteps, then a moment later, Charlie came around the path. He suddenly stopped. "Are you two all right?" he asked. "We heard a holler, and we thought something was wrong."

"Something is very right!" said Peter. "Cassie has agreed to marry me."

"Is that all?" Charlie muttered, and turned away.

Peter chuckled, and Cassie laughed. "Do you suppose Pastor Mike can perform the ceremony?" Peter said.

"Why don't you ask him?" Charlie said over his shoulder.

They did, after supper. When they approached Pastor Mike, he only said, "I've been waiting for this."

Eric agreed. "Now I have a sister and a brother. It's a happy day."

At the next New Beginnings meeting, Pastor Mike shushed everyone, saying they had a special event tonight. Everyone glanced at each other, then became quiet.

The pastor cleared his throat, then said, "It is my great pleasure to announce the engagement of Cassie and Peter. The wedding will take place in one month's time. You are all invited to attend the wedding, and the dinner to follow."

The burst of applause rang through the church.

Epilogue

From the back of the church, Cassie nervously licked her lips once more, waiting for the signal. Pastor Mike stood at the altar, in the front of the church. Peter and Eric were there, as well. Waiting.

The crowd was huge. It pleased her that so many people wanted to see her wed to Peter, including all her school friends. Donna was there, with her husband, and many of the other teachers. Even Rico and his sisters sat in the front row, looking expectant. There were reporters, as well. She'd spotted them as they came in.

Peter had spared no expense on the wedding. A fine catering service hurried even now, to set up dinner down in the hall, with tables in the usual New Beginnings meeting space. Peter had said, "This is the last time I shall ever marry. And it means more to me than mere words. I want everything to be perfect for my bride."

The only thing she'd paid for was her wedding dress. The dress represented all her long-held dreams.

Maggie and Pam, dressed in bridesmaids' dresses of sky blue, peeked from the back room, murmuring words of encouragement to Cassie.

Cassie felt as though she were dreaming. Then a flute began to play. And Ethan's guitar chimed in with the soft wedding march. First Maggie, then Pam walked down the aisle. And finally, Cassie, the bride.

Slowly, she walked down to the front of the church, wearing her long lace gown. She felt radiant. She carried a dozen white roses, around three pure white lilies. They represented the trinity, Peter had said. Something he was just learning about in Bible study.

There, next to Pastor Mike, Peter waited for her, dressed in formal evening dress, as handsome as the day she met him. Yes, he had his faults, but he loved her. And she loved him in return.

Peter waited for her, eyes shining, and open arms ready to hold her. They would hold each other for the rest of their lives, she thought as she glided down the aisle. The sparkle in Peter's eyes told her he was as happy as she. It caused her to catch her breath. Then Peter took her hand, and she heard the words of Pastor Mike. "Dearly beloved, we gather tonight in this assembly to witness the marriage of Peter and Cassie…"

* * * * *

Dear Reader,

Thank you for reading about Cassie and Peter. Loneliness is real. Cassie was lonely, even when her parents were alive. She found compassion and companionship in her church. Do you know anyone like Cassie? Someone who has no family, who never found a mate? Peter is lonely, too, though he doesn't realize it until he's met Cassie. Inviting someone over to visit or to share a meal with you is one way to show you care. As I write this, the Thanksgiving holiday is fast approaching, and we are including one such as Cassie around our dinner table.

May your friends and family surround you with love and care.

Ruth Scofield

QUESTIONS FOR DISCUSSION

1. Cassie cared for her sick father for many years. Why do you think she felt both sadness and relief at his passing? Do you know anyone who is in a similar situation? How did they feel?

2. Determined to overcome her shyness and meet new people, Cassie joins the New Beginnings group at her church. Does she succeed in overcoming her fears? What keeps you from conquering your fears?

3. Peter and Cassie "meet cute" when she spills coffee on him at a New Beginnings meeting. Is Peter sincere in his attentions to Cassie at first? Why or why not?

4. Unhappy with the way she looks, Cassie gradually changes her appearance, with a new hairdo and new clothes. How does this change the rest of her life?

5. Peter disappears for periods of time, then sends Cassie flowers to apologize. Why is Peter so secretive to Cassie about his life? Are you always truthful to the people in your life?

6. Why was Cassie hesitant about traveling to Europe with Peter alone? What would you have done in her place? Would you consider Cassie old-fashioned or just wary?

7. Peter eventually tells Cassie that he once had a son who died from leukemia. Does this revelation tear them apart or bring them closer together? How do you think Peter lived through such a tragedy?

8. Peter and Cassie make an unlikely couple. Do you believe that opposites attract? Like Cinderella, do you think she will live happily ever after with Peter as her Prince Charming?